"We married with the intention of building an alliance—and a family."

Synnamon couldn't argue with this assessment of their marriage—it *had* been far more partnership than passion.

Conner went on calmly. "Then you changed your mind and wanted a divorce, and because that was a decision which affected only the two of us, I went along."

"Exactly," Synnamon agreed. "And we also, if you'll recall, made an agreement to be civilized, amicable, about the whole affair."

"That was before we so *amicably* created a child."

"Conner,' she said desperately, 'you can't force someone to stay married."

His eyes darkened. "Can you honestly tell me, Synnamon, that you love me any less today than you did on our wedding day?"

Leigh Michaels has always loved happy endings. Even when she was a child, if a book's conclusion didn't please her, she'd make up her own. And, though she always wanted to write fiction, she very sensibly planned to earn her living as a newspaper reporter. That career didn't work out, however, and she found herself writing for Harlequin Mills & Boon instead —in the kind of happy ending only a romance novelist could dream up!

Recent titles by the same author:

MARRYING THE BOSS!
BABY, YOU'RE MINE!
THE ONLY SOLUTION
A SINGULAR HONEYMOON

THE PERFECT DIVORCE!

BY

LEIGH MICHAELS

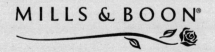

MILLS & BOON®

First published in Great Britain 1997
Harlequin Mills & Boon Limited,
Eton House, 18-24 Paradise Road, Richmond, Surrey, TW9 1SR

This special Reprint Edition is published exclusively
with *Woman's Realm*

© Leigh Michaels 1997

ISBN 0 263 81858 6

Set in Times Roman 10 on 12 pt.
55-9902-54800 C1

Printed and bound in Great Britain
by Caledonian International Book Manufacturing Ltd, Glasgow

CHAPTER ONE

THE Contessa was dying.

Synnamon felt the announcement sinking into her bones like lead into water, and she hardly recognized her own voice. "But I thought she was better! Just last month, after her surgery, she told me—"

The voice at the other end of the telephone line was almost diffident. "I'm sure she didn't want to worry you right then, Mrs. Welles, when you'd just lost your father. But the doctors told her, I believe, that it was only a matter of time."

That made sense, Synnamon thought. With everything that had been going on in Denver in the past few months, it was no wonder the Contessa hadn't wanted to add her bad news to Synnamon's burden.

As if not being prepared would make it easier to lose her, Synnamon thought.

"You won't tell her I called, will you, Mrs. Welles?"

"Of course not, Hartford. I'll be there as soon as I can get on a plane."

She could hear relief in the weary voice. "We'll make arrangements for you and Mr. Welles to be met at the airport."

Synnamon kept her tone steady with an effort. "I don't think Mr. Welles can get away."

There was an instant of shocked silence. "But if you were to come alone, she'd suspect I'd called you. I thought if I could tell her that you and Mr. Welles were coming for a long weekend, sort of sneaking off for a second honeymoon…''

Second honeymoon. If only Hartford knew how deliciously ironic that was! But he was right, of course. The Contessa adored Conner. If he was there, she wouldn't ask uncomfortable questions about exactly why he *wasn't.*

And if there was one thing Synnamon didn't want to explain to her dying godmother, it was that she and Conner would never have a second honeymoon, or even a first anniversary—because in a matter of weeks they'd have a divorce decree, instead.

Synnamon bit her lip and sighed. ''I'll see if he can clear his calendar,'' she said. ''I'll have Annie call you back with the flight number.''

She put the telephone down and noted with detached interest that her hand was trembling. It still looked shockingly bare, too. Though she'd worn her diamond solitaire for less than a year and the matching wedding band for little more than eight months, there hadn't been enough time since she'd taken them off for the indentation at the base of her ring finger to disappear.

She punched the intercom button. ''Annie, book two seats on the first plane to Phoenix, and see if Mrs. Ogden is still at my apartment. If she is, ask her to pack an overnight bag for me, and send a car out to get it. And call Mr. Welles's secretary, please, and ask if he can see me right away.''

Annie's voice held a hint of hesitation. ''Do you want him to come here?''

''Of course not. I'll go to his office. And if there's anything that needs my signature before the end of the week, can you have it ready in the next hour?''

''I'll check, but I'm sure I can.''

''Thanks, Annie.'' Synnamon turned off the intercom

and pulled open the door of her tiny closet to check her hair and makeup. It was silly, perhaps, to still want to look her best for Conner....

Now what had made her think that? She wasn't trying to impress him. It was long-ingrained habit for Synnamon, as the daughter of a cosmetics baron, to always make sure she looked as attractive as possible. And maybe, too, she was trying to postpone the instant she'd have to walk into Conner's office and ask for a major favor.

Which was sillier yet, of course, because in the month since they'd agreed to go their separate ways, they'd gotten along quite well. Not that they'd been pals, exactly—they'd never been that—but they'd discussed their business matters without a hint of acrimony. In fact, Synnamon had almost enjoyed the night they'd had dinner with both their attorneys. They'd been so civilized that they'd settled the entire division of property over the appetizers, and then the four of them had spent the rest of the evening amicably discussing theater and politics.

She straightened her hair, tucking a few ash-blond wisps into the neat French twist, and touched up her mascara even though it was the new brand they were testing—guaranteed to stay on through water aerobics, rainstorms and lifeboat rescues. Then, with nothing else to delay her, Synnamon walked down the hall to the chief executive's office.

The hallways of the Sherwood Cosmetics complex were deeply carpeted in the rich royal blue that was the company's trademark color. Carved into the thick plush at regular intervals was the stylized letter S that Silas Sherwood had sketched on the first lipstick tube he'd manufactured thirty years before.

His monument, Synnamon thought wryly. He'd called it the symbol of an empire built on vanity. Though he'd been talking about the women who used his products, Synnamon had always thought that when it came to defining vanity, her father's own egotism was an even better example.

The marketing director was sitting in the waiting room outside Conner's office, and Synnamon started to take a chair nearby.

But Conner's secretary waved a hand toward the door to the inner office. "Go right on in, Mrs. Welles. He's waiting for you." The surprise in her voice was faint, but Synnamon could hear the signs.

In the time they'd both worked at Sherwood, she'd never been one to pop into Conner's office or encourage him to dash into hers. The rule of business etiquette dictated a polite call before dropping in on a co-worker. She'd seen no reason to violate that rule when the co-worker was her husband, and felt even more strongly about it now that the relationship was in name only. And since Synnamon's job was in customer relations, her business was seldom so urgent that it couldn't wait for the chief executive officer to finish what he was doing and get back to her.

No wonder Carol was surprised today, not only by Synnamon's request for immediate attention but by the fact that Conner had put her ahead of the marketing director.

He's waiting for you. Synnamon wondered if that meant Conner had something on his mind. It must be close to a week since they'd run into each other. Yes, it had been in the staff dining room, last Friday. She'd said a polite hello, and he'd returned it. She'd picked up yogurt and a bagel, and he'd selected a chicken salad plate, and they'd moved almost automatically to tables on opposite sides of the room....

But there couldn't be anything important going on, or

he'd have sought her out and brought it up. They had agreed to be civilized about this whole thing, after all.

Synnamon tapped twice on the door and pushed it open.

The chief executive's office was huge, so big that even the overstuffed couch and love seat seemed to be tucked into a corner. A wall of windows looked out over downtown Denver to the faint blue line of the Rocky Mountains beyond.

Conner was sitting at the enormous ebony and glass table that served as his desk. His profile was silhouetted against the mountain skyline, and the telephone was at his ear.

He looked at Synnamon and murmured into the phone, "Excuse me just a second, Nick."

"I'm sorry." Synnamon's voice was unsteady. "Carol must not have realized you were busy."

"No, I told her to send you in. Sit down, I'll be off in a minute. Ask Carol to bring coffee, if you'd like."

Synnamon shook her head, but Conner didn't seem to notice. He swiveled toward the window and put the phone back to his ear.

She chose the chair squarely across from him and sat down, idly smoothing the rose-pink tweed of her skirt as she watched him. He seemed to have forgotten her presence, or else he was completely undisturbed by it. He'd picked up his conversation crisply, almost in midsentence. Something about the chemical composition of a new product, she thought.

Not that she expected him to be uneasy with her around, any more than she was nervous with him. They were like strangers, really. No, more like longtime casual acquaintances who no longer had much in common. She hadn't even really looked at Conner in weeks—since the day not long after her father's funeral when she'd told him she wanted out of their marriage, out of Sherwood Cosmetics.

Synnamon eased back in her chair, curved one slim leg around the other and watched Conner's profile against the hazy gray-blue of the winter sky. He wasn't conventionally handsome—his face was too craggy for that, his dark hair a little too wiry. But his eyes were quite nice, so blue they were almost purple, surrounded with long black lashes that could turn an ash-blond like Synnamon green with envy. And his smile could be attractive. In fact, just the other day she'd overheard a couple of production-line workers discussing Conner's smile—and other things—in terms that might have made Synnamon blush if she'd still been his wife in anything but the legal sense. *Gorgeous* was one of the terms they'd been tossing around. And *incredibly sexy...*

They were probably right, she admitted calmly, if one was interested in that sort of thing. She could take it or leave it, herself.

She wondered if Carol was the one who made regular appointments for his haircuts these days. Conner certainly was better groomed than before he'd moved into this office.

And the office was different, too, she noticed. The changes since Silas Sherwood's day were subtle—as if Conner were still feeling his way. Or perhaps there were more important things than decorating on his mind. Silas's favorite Andy Warhol print had given way to a soft watercolor of a sailboat passing under a suspension bridge. The overstuffed furniture was the same, but the couch and love seat had been pulled around into a less formal arrangement. The desktop was clear except for a couple of folders, much as Silas had always kept it, but the new coffee table held a bit of clutter, papers Silas would never have allowed to gather. And the putting green that had been her father's favorite tension reliever was gone.

Conner put the telephone down and stood, and for the first time Synnamon realized he was wearing a long white lab coat. That was different, too. She couldn't remember ever seeing her father wearing one, though he had a doctorate in chemistry, just as Conner had. That was one of the reasons, no doubt, that Silas had taken to Conner Welles the moment he'd walked into Sherwood Cosmetics and applied for a job as a research and development chemist.

"What's wrong, Synnamon?"

She must have looked startled, for Conner's eyebrows went up slightly. "I'm not claiming to be psychic," he said dryly. "But when I asked if you'd like to move over to the couch, you didn't hear me. And you've been nibbling at your thumbnail since you came in. Keep it up and you'll have eaten your whole hand by dinnertime."

"Oh." She jerked her hand away from her mouth, feeling color flare in her cheeks. She'd given up biting her nails when she was twelve. What Silas would have said about a relapse didn't bear thinking about—but then she had only herself to please now. "Thanks for seeing me, Conner. I'm sorry to interrupt, and I won't take long, since Larry's waiting outside."

"That's all right—he'll wait."

Synnamon stayed in her chair. She'd completely forgotten what he'd said about moving to the conversational corner, because she was trying to find the words to begin.

After a moment Conner perched on the corner of the glass-topped desk. "I knew if you asked to see me it must be important."

Synnamon searched his voice for sarcasm, but she could find none. Of course not, she told herself. There was no reason for him to be sarcastic. He'd made a simple statement of fact. He knew she wouldn't bother him about trivia.

"It's the Contessa," she said. "Hartford called to tell me she's very ill. He doesn't expect her to survive another week. I'm going to Phoenix this afternoon, as soon as Annie can get me on a plane. And—" She paused and cleared her throat. "Hartford thinks you should come, too."

"He does, does he?" Conner wasn't looking at her but at his shoe, swinging idly back and forth. "What do you think?"

Idiot, she told herself. As if Conner would take his orders from the Contessa's butler! Of course, he wasn't any more likely to take them from Synnamon. Not that she was trying to order him to go to Phoenix, she reminded herself. She was asking a favor, that was all.

"I mean," she went on steadily, "that he doesn't want her to suspect that he's sent for me, which she will if I go alone. And I..."

Conner finished the sentence. "You don't want to tell her about the divorce."

"She's dying, Conner. What good would it do?"

He didn't argue. "Why didn't Hartford tell us before that she was so ill? Or the Contessa herself?"

"She didn't want to worry me."

He looked vaguely dissatisfied. "Why? Are you sure she doesn't know about the divorce?"

"Not from me." Synnamon's voice was sharper than she'd intended, and she regretted it instantly. *You're civilized*, she told herself. *There's no need to shout.* "I intended to go down in a couple of weeks, to break the news to her."

"Well, I certainly haven't told her. I haven't even talked to her."

"I wasn't accusing you. I'm sure she had her reasons for not telling me what the doctors said. They can be wrong, you know."

"But apparently in this case they weren't."

"She might not have wanted to admit it even if she realized the end was coming. Maybe she wants to die with the same grace she's carried all her life, without a whole lot of people standing around her bed."

"And just maybe…" He stopped. "Go on."

"And of course, with my father's heart attack coming just a few weeks before she got this bad news…"

Conner nodded. "That I can understand. But I wouldn't be so certain she doesn't have an inkling what's happening up here. So what's the plan?"

"Hartford wants to tell her we've managed to find a free weekend and we want to get away. The weather's so nice in Phoenix right now that it makes sense." She didn't think there was any point in mentioning what Hartford had said about a second honeymoon. Conner wasn't apt to find any more humor in that than she had.

"And if we both show up, obviously we're still in the throes of love?" Conner didn't sound convinced. "All right. When does the plane leave?"

"Annie's getting tickets. I'll ask her to call Carol with the times." Synnamon slid toward the edge of her chair. "Conner—thanks. This is very kind of you."

For a moment, she thought he wasn't going to answer. "Don't mention it," he said finally. "I'd like to see the Contessa one last time myself."

"I hope it won't interfere too much with your plans."

He shrugged. "Sherwood can run without me for a couple of days."

"That wasn't exactly what I meant. I thought you might have—" she paused and added delicately "—plans for the weekend."

"If that's a request for information about who I'm spending my free time with, Synnamon—"

"It isn't. Not that I'd mind, of course, if you were seeing someone—but I'd be sorry about your plans. I just want you to know that I appreciate how civilized you're being about this."

"From you, my dear," Conner said, "that is the highest compliment possible."

The flight seemed to take forever. Synnamon turned down the snack the attendant offered and stared out the window as she sipped her glass of white wine, trying to ignore Conner in the seat beside her. Not that he was attempting to gain her attention. That was obvious. He philosophically munched his airline peanuts, drank a single Scotch and water, and then leaned back, eyes closed, arms folded across his broad chest.

Synnamon had no idea if he was napping, meditating or contemplating a complex chemical formula, and she didn't care. She wasn't bothered by his presence, either, not really. It was just that he seemed to occupy all the space and consume all the air in the cabin. Thank heaven Annie had booked them into first class. Synnamon hated to think what this flight would have been like if Conner had had to fold his six-feet-four into a narrow coach seat. She'd have been practically sitting in his lap.

She hadn't been so close to him since her father's funeral, and that day she'd been too numb to notice much. She remembered that he'd been unobtrusively beside her every minute, offering an arm for support. She hadn't needed it, of course, but it had been some comfort to know he was there.

And it would help to have him there when she saw the Contessa, too. The Contessa had fallen in love with Conner at first sight, and he could help bridge any awkward gaps that might arise. It wasn't going to be easy to see a woman she loved in the state Hartford had implied....

Synnamon sighed.

Conner didn't open his eyes. "I'd suggest you wait till you get there to start mourning."

Synnamon stared at him. His lashes, long and thick and black, lay heavily against high, strong cheekbones. "That's a pretty heartless attitude."

The seat belt sign came on, and Conner shrugged and sat up straight. "Not really. I was just imagining the Contessa flinging open the front door and saying, *Surprise!*"

"The Contessa would never go along with such a cruel practical joke, much less plan it. Besides, why would she have Hartford tell me she's dying if she's not?" Synnamon handed her half-full wineglass to the flight attendant and returned her seat to the upright position.

"Because that announcement got us both down here. And if my suspicions are right and she wants to have a little talk about our marriage—"

"Our marriage—our *former* marriage—is none of the Contessa's business."

"You can try that line on her. As the former advice queen of the nation, she might see things differently."

"Etiquette was her specialty, not straightening out the lovelorn. Has anyone ever told you you're a cynic, Conner?" Below the plane, the city of Phoenix spread out almost to the mountain ranges that surrounded the flat valley. The minutes were ticking by, and Synnamon's heart began to pound. "What if I don't know what to say to her?'' She wasn't talking to him so much as to herself. ''I've never seen anybody who was dying…except for my father, of course. But he went so suddenly that there wasn't time to think about it.''

''Silas never did have any patience with being kept waiting,'' Conner said.

Synnamon bit her lip. That was typical, she thought. It wasn't often she forgot herself enough to confide her fears, but when she did, the answer was glib. Just as it would have been if it had been Silas instead of Conner beside her—except, she thought, she'd never seen any indication that Silas possessed a sense of humor.

She turned toward the window once more. The pitch of the engines changed as the runway rose to meet them, and the slight vertigo she always experienced on landings rocked her stomach.

''Synnamon.''

She didn't look at him. ''What?''

''Follow her lead.'' His voice was almost somber. ''If she wants to talk about dying, let her. If she doesn't, tell her what you remember most—remind her of the good times you had together.''

Synnamon hesitated, then nodded. But she didn't turn away from the window, and a moment later the plane's tires screeched against the runway.

A uniformed chauffeur was waiting at the gate with a sign that said Welles. Synnamon handed him her overnight case, and he led the way across the terminal to a white Cadillac limousine.

Conner raised an eyebrow. ''Do you ever consider taking the middle-class way, Synnamon? Like a taxi?''

''What good would that do?''

''A rhetorical question if I ever heard one.'' He handed

his bag to the chauffeur and opened the back door of the car for Synnamon.

As the chauffeur slid behind the wheel, she leaned forward to make sure he had the Contessa's address. She braced her left hand on the jump seat and swore under her breath when she realized that her finger was still bare. "My rings," she said. "I forgot all about the rings, and no matter how sick she is, that's exactly the kind of little touch the Contessa is bound to notice. I suppose I can tell her they're at the jewelers being cleaned, but—"

Conner reached into the inside breast pocket of his blazer and dropped a small black velvet bag into her palm. "I wondered when you'd remember."

Synnamon tipped the contents into her hand. Even in the subdued light that passed through the limousine's tinted windows, the full-carat diamond solitaire flashed fire, and the matching wedding band, crusted with tiny stones, sparkled like a fresh snowfall. Almost reluctantly, she slid them onto her finger, the wedding band first, closest to her heart as tradition dictated, and then the solitaire to stand guard.

"I wouldn't have thought you'd have time to get them," she said. "But of course if you went home to pack—"

Or perhaps he'd kept them closer at hand.

But why would he? The rings were no more pleasant a memory to Conner than they were to Synnamon. It was a foolish idea, probably born of the fact that the platinum bands were warm from his body—as if that meant he'd carried them for the past month. The truth was, until this instant she wouldn't even have bet that he'd kept them.

Almost as if he'd read her mind, Conner said, "They were in the office safe. It's a whole lot more secure than leaving them in a hotel room. And I didn't have to go back to the hotel to pack. I've gotten in the habit of keeping some clothes in the office.''

''That's certainly handy,'' Synnamon said crisply.

Conner shot a sideways look at her. ''What does that mean?''

''Nothing. My father obviously thought it was a good idea, or he wouldn't have built a closet and a dressing room into his executive bath. That's all.''

''Well, it's one thing Silas was right about. How did you manage to pack, anyway?''

''I didn't. Mrs. Ogden threw some things together, and one of the couriers made a detour and picked my bag up.''

''What will you do after the end of the year, Synnamon, when you don't have all of Sherwood's resources to draw on any more?''

She looked at him levelly. ''Are you afraid I'll still demand perks after I leave the company? Don't worry about me, Conner. Even after our division of property, I won't exactly be poverty-stricken.'' Deliberately, she changed the subject. ''Mrs. Ogden asked about you just this morning, by the way. I think she misses you.''

''How kind of her. Perhaps when I get an apartment she'll come to take care of me on the days she's not working for you.''

Was he serious? But why shouldn't he be? ''That would be tidy,'' she agreed. ''Of course, I have her come in most days, so she doesn't have much time left for anyone else. Why are you still living in the hotel, anyway?''

Conner shrugged. ''When you're starting from scratch, it takes time to find an apartment and furniture and appliances.''

And he'd given up most of his things when they'd married. Not that he'd had much, Synnamon thought, so if he was suggesting it was her fault he had nothing in the way of household goods...

But of course he wasn't. She'd asked him, over the appetizers the night they'd agreed to terms, if he wanted anything in their apartment, and he'd made it clear he didn't.

The limousine purred through traffic, smoothly negotiating the beginnings of rush hour, and pulled up at a wrought-iron gate. Beyond it lay a long, curving row of elegant town houses, set at angles that increased the sense of privacy, each surrounded by a lawn so plush and unusually green—given the desert surroundings—that the grass looked artificial.

The guard at the gate checked his list and passed them through, and the limousine pulled up smoothly in front of the Contessa's home.

Thought it was technically a town house, Synnamon had always thought it was more like a villa. This was no mere two-level apartment, as most town houses were. It spread out lavishly at the end of the complex, and the front door, behind a colonnaded entrance, silently invited them to approach.

After the gray day they'd left in Denver and the tinted windows of the limousine, the Phoenix sunshine was harsh and brilliant. Synnamon stood for a moment outside the car, blinking, not quite sure if it was sunlight or tears that made her eyes hurt.

Conner signed the limousine bill and joined her on the sidewalk. "You know," he said, "you never have told me how the Contessa got her name."

He was trying to distract her, Synnamon knew. It was kind of him to bother. "It started as a joke when she was a child," she said. "She was the elegant one in a big and rowdy Italian family. Some of her brothers and sisters called her prissy. Then when she grew up and became the arbiter of proper behavior—not quite as famous as Emily Post, of course, but just as respected and obeyed—she cultivated the image of the Contessa. Now hardly anyone remembers her real name.''

Synnamon took a deep breath and braced herself as the front door opened, revealing a woman in her sixties wearing a black dress and a crisp white apron.

The woman's eyes were swollen and red, and her lower lip trembled. ''Oh, Mrs. Welles,'' she said, her voice shaking. ''I'm so glad you're here!'' She held out her arms, and Synnamon took a step forward and gathered the woman close.

Over her shoulder, she cast a glance at Conner, who looked a bit subdued. So much for his expectations that the Contessa herself would greet them, in perfect health and high spirits at having pulled off a prank.

But Synnamon had to admit that despite her knowledge of the Contessa she'd been hoping against hope Conner might be right. Now that last flicker of wishful thinking faded into darkness, and a chill settled deep in her heart.

She patted Mrs. Hartford on the shoulder and looked over the woman's head toward the butler, hovering in the hallway. ''Take us to her, please, Hartford,'' she said. ''We've left it too long as it is.''

Midnight found her beside the Contessa's bed. A favorite book from her childhood lay open on her lap, but it had been long minutes since Synnamon had looked at the pages. She was watching the Contessa instead, searching the dear and familiar face, studying each line, each shadow and trying to figure out which ones were new. The Contessa's skin had always been luminous. Now it was almost translucent. Her eyelids, closed in a shallow sleep, seemed paper-thin. Her breath was faint. Her thin body seemed so fragile that Synnamon feared even the weight of the blanket might crush her.

As if there had been no interruption in the conversation, the Contessa sighed and said, "I'm so sorry, my darling. You came for a weekend getaway, and I'm ruining it. I can't help being glad to have you here, but it's terribly rude of me to spoil your holiday."

Synnamon couldn't keep herself from smiling at the slightly querulous tone. The voice of conscience, Synnamon had called it in her youth.

Mrs. Hartford came in with a medicine cup and a glass of water, and the Contessa waved a fragile hand toward the door. "Don't let me be so selfish, Synnamon. Go to your husband now. That's where you belong." Her hand dropped as if the effort had exhausted her.

Mrs. Hartford nodded. "She'll sleep for a while," she said softly. "And I'll sit with her."

Synnamon knew better than to argue. Perhaps the Contessa would rest more easily if she wasn't trying to talk. "You'll call me if she wants me." It wasn't a question.

"Of course. Or Hartford will—he's sleeping now, but he'll take over in a few hours."

Synnamon walked slowly across the balcony that divided the Contessa's bedroom from the guest quarters, pausing to look down into the enormous living room below. The scent of roses, freshly arranged in a crystal vase on the baby grand piano, tugged at her senses. She wondered when Mrs. Hartford had found the time for flowers, but she knew why she'd managed it. The Contessa loved roses—and if she gathered enough strength to walk out of her room again, there would be roses waiting for her.

Synnamon was still holding the book she'd been reading to the Contessa. She looked at the intricately drawn leaves on the cover and remembered what the Contessa had said when Synnamon had opened it to the first chapter.

"*The Secret Garden*," she'd murmured. "I feel somehow that I'll see that garden very soon."

Synnamon closed her eyes for a moment and swallowed hard, and then walked deliberately across to the guest suite. She did her best to be quiet, in case Conner was already asleep.

But the lights were on, and he was lying atop one of the twin beds, reading the *Wall Street Journal*. The spread had been turned back, but he hadn't bothered to get between the sheets. He'd simply stretched out across the blankets.

Perhaps, Synnamon thought, that was because he wasn't exactly dressed for bed. He was wearing jogging shorts and a T-shirt, as if he'd expected to be summoned to the Contessa's room. Or maybe it was all he had. No doubt Conner didn't keep pajamas in his office closet any more than Silas had. Though there had been talk about Silas sleeping in his office....

She noted and tried to ignore Conner's long, strong legs, the powerful breadth of his chest, the muscular arms under the short sleeves of the tight shirt, and turned toward the rack at the foot of the other bed, where Hartford had placed her overnight bag.

Twin beds. She almost hadn't noticed.

Well, that was a benefit she hadn't counted on. The last time they'd visited the Contessa—the only time the two of them had shared this room, shortly after their wedding—the beds had been pushed together and made up as a single king-size unit.

"How is she?" Conner asked.

"Worn out—and fading, I'm afraid, even since you saw

her. I think Hartford was optimistic when he said it might be a week.''

''I'm sorry,'' he said gently.

Synnamon nodded. She couldn't say anything. She was afraid if she tried she'd break down.

The only nightgown she could find in her bag was the flimsiest and laciest she owned. Mrs. Ogden's doing, of course—the woman loved lacy lingerie. That, Synnamon thought, would teach her to be catty about Conner's lack of pajamas!

By the time she came out of the bathroom, he'd turned off the light above his bed, leaving only the small lamp near hers, and the moonlight that filtered through the sheer curtains, to illuminate the room.

Synnamon slid between the sheets and turned off the lamp.

It was almost worse than being alone, to know that he was across the room. In the dark, the demons seemed to grow and taunt her, and she couldn't even cry, or he would know.

She was losing the most precious person in her world, the one who had always understood and loved her no matter what. The Contessa hadn't been required by the bonds of family to love Synnamon. She'd *chosen* to care about her—and that made her more valuable than anyone else had ever been.

Now—in a day, maybe two, but certainly not much longer—Synnamon would be entirely alone in the world.

The tears started as a silent trickle and grew into a flood. And though she tried fiercely to be quiet, the sobs could not be smothered. They wrenched at her chest, at her throat, at her heart.

''Synnamon,'' he said, and she heard his footsteps, soft as they were on the deep carpet. His hand passed over her hair, so tentatively that she could barely feel his touch—but it seemed as if his gentle gesture had reached deep inside her and flipped a switch.

She reached for him, tugging him down to her, as if by holding onto Conner she could cling to all that was sweet and precious in her life and keep it from slipping away.

"Hold me," she whispered. "Help me forget."

"Are you sure you know what you're asking, Synnamon?"

"I'm sure."

Slowly, his palm cupped her chin and turned her face, and he bent his head as if to kiss her temple. A kiss of pity, she thought—not at all what she needed just now. She twisted frantically in his arms till his lips, instead of brushing the corner of her eye, met hers like sparks striking gunpowder.

She could taste his strength, his warmth, his desire. He couldn't hide the truth, that in this instant he wanted *her*—only her—and the knowledge fed her longing.

"Make me forget it all, Conner," she said against his mouth. "Everything."

He didn't make her forget…at least, not quite. Perhaps nothing could have done that. But by the time the world exploded around her, the pain of impending loss had receded to a thin shadow at the corners of her mind, overwhelmed by the pure sensuality of his touch, the fire of his fingertips against her skin, the velvet of his lips against hers, the whisper of two bodies communicating in the wordless language men and women created long before the dawn of time.

He held her, afterward, the two of them curled together on the single narrow bed. Neither of them spoke.

With her body still throbbing, Synnamon forced herself

to lie still, to breathe normally, to stay quiet, to pretend to sleep.

But deep inside her mind, as the shadows crept back, she was shrieking, *What have I done*?

CHAPTER TWO

THE sky was starting to lighten when Hartford knocked on the door of the guest suite to summon them, and before full daylight the Contessa had gone into the secret garden she had talked of, where her beloved roses would never fade or lose their scent.

Synnamon stayed beside the bed for a long time, hands folded, watching the still, peaceful face. When she finally came downstairs, Conner was sitting at the grand piano, picking out a melancholy one-fingered melody. Without a word, he moved across the room to a silver tray on a low table and poured her a cup of coffee.

She held it, hardly feeling the heat radiating through the china and sinking into her fingers. "Perhaps you'd call the airline," she said finally. "I can be ready to go in an hour or so."

Conner frowned. "Go where?"

"Denver. Home. Where else?"

"But what about the arrangements?" he asked quietly.

"The Contessa took care of that long ago." Synnamon smiled a little, but it took all the strength she had. "She had definite views on the rudeness of leaving that sort of job for someone else to do. And since she didn't want any sort of funeral service, just cremation with her ashes scattered in…" Her voice began to tremble as the reality once more hit home.

She half-expected Conner to reach for her, or at least to extend a hand. Her body tightened, and embarrassment flooded over her at the memory of her uninhibited behavior last night. The way she had responded to him, demanded, pleaded, begged...

But Conner didn't move. He simply stood quietly in the center of the Contessa's elegant living room, looking at her.

Thank heaven, Synnamon thought, *he's sensitive enough to understand that last night was an aberration.*

"Are you certain you want to go home just now?" Conner asked. "I should get back, I suppose, but there's really no reason for you to rush."

Synnamon shook her head quickly. "Oh, no. I'll be better if I'm busy." Too late, she realized that meant she'd be flying back with him. How easy it would have been to wait till tomorrow, or even to take a later plane today.

Had he meant that he didn't want her to come along? Surely not, she told herself. The flight would be so brief it couldn't matter, and then they would both be free to plunge into their jobs, into real life. "Besides," she went on firmly, "the Hartfords need a rest, not someone else to take care of."

"I'm not sure they'd agree with you. They might even like the distraction. I think I actually hurt Hartford's feelings this morning by telling him not to bother with breakfast." Conner pointed at the cup in her hand. "Drinking that, instead of only holding it, might do you good, Synnamon."

"And if I don't drink my coffee, Hartford will really be hurt?" Obediently she raised the cup to her lips. He'd put in half a spoon of sugar, exactly the way she liked it. She was vaguely surprised, until she realized that if the roles had been reversed she'd have remembered how to fix his, too—with just a touch of cream.

"Well, I wouldn't be surprised if they both feel a bit threatened just now."

Synnamon shook her head. "The Contessa arranged a pension plan. And I've already told them they can stay here as long as they like."

"You'll keep the town house, then?"

"Oh, yes. I can't imagine dividing up her things...." Her voice began to shake again, despite her best efforts, and she had to take a couple of deep breaths before she could say, "I just want to go home."

"Synnamon..." He paused. "I'll call the airline."

She set her cup on the silver tray and tugged the rings from her finger. "Here," she said as she held them out to him. "So I don't forget them later."

Slowly, Conner raised a hand to take the gleaming bands from her. "Are you sure this is a good idea?"

She frowned. "Why not? I doubt the Hartfords will notice. And they'll have to know about the divorce sometime, anyway. Now that the Contessa's gone..." She drew her elbows close against her body. "Conner, I want to thank you for—" she hesitated "—for consoling me last night. I'll be fine, really."

He said levelly, "I'm sure you will." He looked at the rings, the stones sparkling against his palm. "I always thought diamonds were perfect for you, Synnamon, but I wasn't quite sure why. Now I know. They're every bit as brilliant and hard as you are."

Synnamon toyed with a bread stick and tried not to look out the window. A mid-December snowstorm was venting its fury on Denver, and from twenty stories above the street, atop one of the city's premier hotels, all she could see was a gray-white cloud that shifted and rolled and twisted till her stomach threatened to rebel. To make it worse, the Pinnacle was a revolving restaurant, and though the constant and slightly jerky motion normally didn't bother her, today she felt like she'd been stranded on a carnival ride.

But the restaurant was her attorney's favorite, and when Morea had called yesterday to set up a lunch date so they could talk about the progress of the divorce, Synnamon hadn't hesitated to accept the invitation. Of course yesterday she hadn't been thinking about the predicted snow.

Morosely, she snapped another bread stick in two and played with it. The wind seemed to whistle around the glass and steel tower.

The maître d' swept across the room and with a flourish pulled out the chair opposite Synnamon's. Morea Landon settled into place with a sigh, tossed the end of a fringed red silk scarf over her shoulder with an elegant flourish and leaned forward to touch Synnamon's hand. "Darling, how are you?" Her voice was low and husky. "I haven't seen you in two weeks, at least."

"I'd be better if it wasn't snowing horizontally."

Morea smiled sympathetically and glanced at her menu for all of three seconds before tossing it aside. "It does look a bit like a Rorschach test out there, doesn't it? Want to split a bottle of wine?"

"No, thanks. I'm dizzy enough with the rotation and the snow."

"Club soda, then. And turn your back to the window. Or else watch the snow more closely—that might help. I remember my dad got me used to thunderstorms by treating them like a video game and making me tell him what I thought the lightning looked like."

"Sort of like searching out pictures in the clouds?"

"Exactly. See that little eddy right there? It resembles the governor on a bad hair day, don't you think?" She sobered. "I'm dreadfully sorry about the Contessa, Synnamon."

"Thanks for the note you sent."

"You were planning to go down for Christmas, weren't you?"

"Actually, I'd planned to be there about now. I didn't want to break bad news to her on the holiday." Synnamon glanced at her menu, more for the sake of a moment to reassert her self-control than because she needed to refresh her memory, and looked at the waiter. "I'll have the seafood salad, with house dressing."

"And I'll have the scampi with a double order of garlic toast." Morea smiled sweetly. "I'm spending the afternoon in conference with my opponent in a divorce case that is not likely to be as easily settled as yours. I figure he might be more willing to negotiate if it's the only way he can escape the garlic."

"Is that what they teach you in law school?"

"Oh, no. In law school I only learned which books to look things up in." Morea raised her glass of club soda. "I have a date for you, finally. Here's to your divorce, which will be final in the middle of February. On the fourteenth, to be precise."

Synnamon almost dropped her glass. "Valentine's Day? But that's—"

"Your wedding anniversary, I know. At least it's tidy," Morea pointed out. "You'll never have any trouble remembering the date of your freedom. And you can go to the Valentine's Have a Heart Ball as a single woman with an absolutely clear conscience."

"I doubt I'll be celebrating," Synnamon murmured.

Morea set her glass down. Her voice was suddenly serious. "Look, darling, if you have any doubts about whether this divorce is what you want—"

"Of course I don't have doubts. It's the only answer. This marriage was a big mistake for both of us."

"Well, you're probably half right."

"What does that mean?"

"Conner's come out of the whole thing rather well, hasn't he? You know, Synnamon, you don't have to give him the earth wrapped in gold tissue paper in order to get out of this marriage. If you want to fight to keep what's yours—"

"All I want is a clean, fair finish."

"That," Morea murmured, "is exactly what I'm talking about. Especially the *fair* part."

Synnamon ignored the comment. "It's not as if Conner doesn't have any right to Sherwood Cosmetics. My father made him president of the company and a full partner."

"Silas was an idiot. Besides, that doesn't mean you have to meekly hand over the rest."

"I'm not. I'll still have a good share of Sherwood when it's done, as well as the apartment and everything in it. Morea, whose side are you on, anyway?"

"Yours, darling—and the little oath I swore when I passed the bar was to give you, my client, my very best advice."

"Consider it done, all right? My mind's made up."

The waiter brought their food. Synnamon picked up her fork, but somehow the salad—as delightful as it had sounded—wasn't inviting any more. The scallops piled atop the bed of lettuce seemed to quiver with the motion of the restaurant. They almost looked alive, Synnamon thought.

Morea crunched a crisp bit of garlic toast with evident delight. "I can't wait to see Ridge Coltrain's face when he gets a load of this," she murmured. "Best garlic toast in the world. So, if we're finished talking about the divorce, what are we to discuss? Oh, I know—what are you doing for Christmas? If you're not going to Phoenix, why not come and celebrate with us?''

"I didn't say I wasn't going to Phoenix," Synnamon said.

Morea frowned. "You didn't? I'd have sworn...."

Synnamon relented. "Actually, I'm not. But I've already made plans for Christmas Day."

The fact that her plans included staying quietly at home alone, sleeping late and watching old movies was really none of Morea's business. As the Contessa would have said, as long as one didn't actually lie, there was no need to tell the entire truth on every occasion. And in a case like this, Synnamon would much rather be alone than at the fringes of Morea's crowd, where everyone seemed to be half of a twosome.

"With somebody interesting, I hope? Maybe it's a good thing after all that you and Conner are being so decent about the whole thing. If one of you wanted to make a fuss about who the other one's seeing, it could get rather unpleasant."

"Why? Who's Conner seeing?" The words were out before Synnamon could stop herself.

Morea wagged a gentle index finger at her.

"Not that I care, you understand," Synnamon said.

"Of course not. In any case, how should I know? I hear things now and then, but I haven't seen Conner since the night we all had dinner together and you practically shoved money at him. Not that I'm trying to reargue the case now," Morea added hastily. "It's just been a long time since I've had a client who was more interested in giving property away than in keeping it."

"Morea—"

"Bear with me, darling. In another eight weeks the divorce will be final, and I promise I'll shut up about it forever after. But in the meantime, just in case you change your mind, I want you to know where I stand. Just don't wait too long, all right?'' She stabbed a shrimp. ''Now then. If you won't come for turkey, how about later? A bunch of us are going up to Telluride the week after Christmas. If you don't feel like skiing, you can always sit in the whirlpool and flirt with all the hunks who get hurt on the slopes.''

''Thanks, but that's the last week I'll be working, so I think I'd better stick around the office. Conner still hasn't hired anybody to take over my job, so—''

''Does he run the rest of the business with the same degree of foresight and care? No wonder Silas thought he was perfect.''

Synnamon couldn't help but bristle a bit. ''Don't be sarcastic, Morea. It's not Conner's fault the job hasn't been filled.''

''I'm charmed to hear you defending him.''

''He turned the interviews and the decision over to me, and I haven't found anybody who's really qualified.'' She pushed her salad away. ''In fact, I have an appointment to talk to him this afternoon about that.''

''Are you sure you want to give up your job?'' Morea asked idly.

''Oh, yes. I've been in customer relations since I joined Sherwood three years ago, and I'm a little tired of it.''

''No doubt. Who wouldn't be, dealing with complaints all day? What I really meant was that perhaps you just want a change. You should have had the top job, you know, instead of Conner.''

''Me? Why?''

''Well, you *are* the only remaining Sherwood.''

''You think that mattered to my father? He never

thought I could do anything.'' Synnamon regretted letting the bitter tone ooze into her voice, and she masked it as quickly as she could. ''That's partly why I didn't mind giving so much of my share of the company to Conner. If he's going to have all the responsibility—''

''I still think it was foolish of you. Conner's got a majority interest in a very profitable cosmetics firm. And you've got—''

''A nice guaranteed income, without working another day in my life.''

''So what are you going to do instead?''

''I'm not sure. Maybe I'll grow poinsettias.''

Morea sighed. ''Well, at least make it pink ones, darling. Red's the wrong color for you. Or won't you take my advice on that, either?''

At one minute to three, Synnamon took a seat in the waiting room outside Conner's office. ''It's going to be a while,'' Carol warned. ''He's pretty thoroughly tied up.''

''I'll wait.'' Synnamon opened her portfolio and started through the stack of applications again.

It was a full twenty minutes before the office door opened and the head of the research and development division came out, stopped to shake Conner's hand, nodded to Synnamon and went off down the hall.

Conner leaned against the doorjamb and sighed. Then he said, ''Sorry I'm running late, Synnamon. Come on in. Carol, I could use a cup of coffee, after that.''

Synnamon pushed the applications into her portfolio. ''Problems with research and development?''

''You might say.'' He closed the office door behind her and gestured toward the couch in the corner. ''Anderson just announced his intention of retiring at the end of the year.''

"You mean this year? That's a bit abrupt—it's only two weeks off." Taking a seat on the couch could be interpreted as issuing an invitation. Synnamon chose the love seat instead. She sat in the precise center and put her portfolio on the low glass table.

"It does add a little extra spice to the holidays, having to decide who gets the job. Oh, well, I wasn't planning to go anywhere for Christmas, anyway."

"I suppose you'll be promoting one of the senior people?"

"They're all well-qualified."

"I know."

Conner settled onto the end of the couch and stretched one arm across the back. "But you sound a bit doubtful."

"Not really. It's just that some of those people have been with the company for twenty years—almost as long as Anderson has. Perhaps some new blood would be a good idea."

Conner frowned, but just as he started to answer, Carol knocked and wheeled in a small cart. By the time she'd poured the coffee and gone out, Synnamon had thought better of the impulse to express her opinion. In two more weeks, she, too, would be leaving Sherwood Cosmetics. After that she'd be no more than a silent partner, so she'd better get used to keeping her ideas to herself.

Not that it would be a difficult change, she thought. Silas Sherwood had certainly never solicited her opinion. In fact, the main difference between Conner and her father was that Silas wouldn't have bothered to listen before doing exactly as he pleased.

She stirred sugar into her coffee and leaned forward to open her portfolio. "But of course you're the boss. As you requested, I've brought a list of the best applicants for my job." She frowned at the neatly typed page atop the stack of applications. "The trouble is, none of them are all that good. The top candidate was so busy assuring me of his qualifications that he never let me tell him about the job. I suspect he'd be like that with our clients, too, not even listening to their needs."

"Not the kind of customer service we want to provide," Conner agreed. "I see your point. What do you want to do? Run the ad again?"

"No." Synnamon took a deep breath. "You may think this is shortsighted—"

Conner shook his head. "No—Anderson giving me two weeks' notice is shortsighted. Knowing you, Synnamon, I can't imagine you'd make a proposition without having figured out every possible consequence."

She wasn't quite sure if she'd been complimented or insulted, but she decided not to test the question. "I want to hire Annie."

Conner's eyebrows flew up. "Your secretary?"

The incredulity in his voice reminded her painfully of Silas, and she had to fight the urge to duck her head and apologize for having wasted his time. "She's already half-trained for the job," she pointed out.

"That's quite a promotion, don't you think?"

"Yes, and I think she could handle it beautifully. But of course the decision is yours."

He leaned back against the cushions, long fingers stroking the strong line of his jaw, watching her thoughtfully.

Synnamon waited patiently for rejection, wondering what reason—if any—he would give. Why had she even bothered? Secretaries didn't get promoted to department head status in one leap.

Abruptly Conner rose, walked across the room to his desk and keyed the intercom. "Carol, ask Mrs. Welles's secretary to come to my office immediately."

Synnamon blinked in surprise. "You mean—"

"Let's wait till Annie gets here, shall we?"

Chastened, Synnamon sipped her coffee. The silence lengthened uncomfortably, and finally she said, "Morea told me the divorce will be final in about eight weeks."

Conner looked thoughtful. "Valentine's Day," he said.

It hadn't taken him long to calculate that. Synnamon wondered if Morea was right and he was seeing someone already.

I don't care if he is, she told herself. *It's curiosity, that's all.*

There was a tentative tap on the door and Annie came in. She looked, Synnamon thought, like a kid who'd been summoned to the principal's office and didn't have the slightest idea why. "You wanted to see me, Mr. Welles?"

"Have a seat, Annie. How do you like your coffee?"

Annie perched on the edge of the love seat next to Synnamon. "Just black, thanks."

He handed her a cup and saucer. It rattled a little as she took it, and she didn't even pretend to drink.

Conner settled back on the couch. "Mrs. Welles has found the person she feels is just right to take over her job."

"Yes, sir?"

"You."

The saucer tipped alarmingly. "I— Me, sir?" Annie cleared her throat. "Sir, I know I should jump at the chance. But I'm not sure—"

"Exactly," Conner said. "I'm not sure, either. Annie, I have a proposition for you, if Mrs. Welles will go along with it."

Warning bells went off in Synnamon's head, but before she could argue, he'd gone on. He wasn't even looking at her, but directly at Annie.

"I'm offering you the job as head of customer relations on a trial basis for a ninety-day period. During that time, Mrs. Welles will make herself available to you for advice and consultation."

Synnamon gave him a stony stare.

"At the end of the trial period," Conner went on, "the three of us will sit down again and decide if the plan is working. If it is, we'll make the promotion permanent."

And if not, Synnamon thought, *it's quite apparent whose neck will be on the line.*

"Is that agreeable to you both?" Conner asked.

Synnamon nodded curtly. She could hardly disagree, since it had been her idea. Though what could he do to her, after all, if Annie failed? And Annie wouldn't fail.

Conner said, "Then let's shake hands on it." He extended a hand to Annie, and then to Synnamon.

There was no way to politely refuse, though she wanted to. She hadn't touched him since that night in Phoenix when she'd thrown herself at him with such embarrassing abandon. On the flight to Denver they hadn't even sat together. The plane had been almost full—but she'd wondered at the time if he'd arranged the separate seats on purpose.

His hand was firm and warm, the palm as smooth against hers as it had been against her breast that night almost four weeks ago—

And that is enough of that, she told herself. The sooner that night was entirely forgotten, the better.

She stood up. "If that's all, Conner, Annie and I have a lot of work to do."

He smiled. "No particular hurry. You have ninety days, Synnamon, so surely you can take a minute to finish your coffee."

*　　*　　*

Christmas had a habit of never going quite as one expected, Synnamon thought. She was alone, just as she'd planned. The telephone was quiet, as she'd planned. Her nontraditional holiday feast was spread out on the glass-topped dining room table, as she'd planned—caviar and pâté and quails' eggs carefully arranged on a picture-perfect plate.

But the only thing that looked good was the toast points.

"Isn't it just my luck," she said, "to have to share Christmas dinner with a virus?"

She munched a bit of toast and stared at the only ornament in the apartment, a big glass ball Annie had painted to look like carved marble. It looked terribly lonely, perched on an antique salt cellar in the middle of the dining room table.

"I know you're not much in the mood to celebrate this year," the secretary had said when she'd brought it into Synnamon's office last week. "But I wanted you to have a reminder that I'll be thinking about you. And if you change your mind and want to come over, just call."

It was a good thing she hadn't, though, Synnamon thought. Annie had two small children, and she wouldn't want to give this virus to them. It was funny, though, how this thing seemed to come and go. She could be exhausted and miserably nauseated—and half an hour later feel energetic enough to go dancing.

She picked up the marbleized ornament and cradled it in her hand. This would certainly be a Christmas to remember—despite her best efforts to make it completely forgettable.

"And that's quite enough feeling sorry for yourself," she said firmly. "It was your decision to be alone, after all."

And not just for today, either, but altogether. She didn't doubt that if she hadn't asked for her freedom, things would be going along now just as they had for the first six months she and Conner had been married. All very pleasant and decent, but…lacking. The trouble was, she didn't quite know what was missing.

The holidays had never been the season of shimmering happiness for Synnamon that they seemed to be for other people. Last Christmas, with a brand-new diamond solitaire sparkling on her ring finger, she'd had hopes of feeling that incredible joy.

But the day had turned out much the same as every other holiday she could remember. She and Conner had had dinner with Silas. The men had talked business till she'd wanted to scream, and when she'd excused herself to retreat to the kitchen, they hadn't even seemed to notice. But Silas's housekeeper, horrified at her request for something to do, had shooed her back to the living room. Silas had eventually remembered it was Christmas and handed her the usual envelope with the usual sizeable check.…

No, she couldn't regret not having a repetition of that. The trouble was, she wasn't so sure what she wanted instead.

Today, with Silas gone, she and Conner would probably have gone to one of the country clubs for the luncheon buffet. A holiday dinner just for them was too much trouble, and Mrs. Ogden wanted the holiday with her own family, anyway, instead of with her employers.

But next year, Synnamon thought, she'd put up a tree no matter what. She might even cook a turkey—who cared if it was just for herself? At least, she'd make a stab at having a normal Christmas, the kind Annie and other people talked about.

Her stomach protested the idea of food, and she had to swallow hard to keep it in place. Hoping to distract herself, she wandered through the big living room and down the hall, as if she was seeing the apartment for the first time.

The apartment was too big for one person. It had been large even for the two of them. But then she'd expected that someday there'd be a child.

Synnamon had chosen the apartment, but it had been Silas's wedding gift, and she'd had as much fun decorating and furnishing as if she'd been outfitting a full-size dollhouse. She hadn't realized till later that Conner hadn't seemed especially interested in any of it.

She opened the door to his den for the first time in weeks. It was still as perfect as the day she'd put the final touches in place. It smelled like leather and—despite Mrs. Ogden's constant cleaning—just a little like stale dust. He'd never really used it. He'd never even seemed to live here. Last fall, when he'd moved out, he'd taken only his clothes. Nothing else had changed. It was as if he'd been only a visitor in her home, in her life.

That might have hurt, if she'd ever been foolish enough to believe that Conner had fallen in love with her. But he was too much like her father for that. She'd found that chemists were something like engineers—levelheaded and logical, wanting everything to have a sensible explanation.

No, Conner's behavior had never been that of a young man in love. But then she'd never expected it to be. She'd always been aware that any man would find himself at least as attracted to Sherwood Cosmetics as he was to Synnamon herself. If she'd needed any further evidence of that, she'd have found it in Silas's reaction to the news of her engagement. He'd been delighted, excited beyond anything he'd ever expressed before—at least where Synnamon was concerned. And before the week was out he'd announced that Conner would be his successor as president of the company.

Their marriage might have been a chilly sort of bargain, but Synnamon had seen no reason they couldn't make it work. Even the Contessa had told her, through the years, that love was greatly overrated, that there was a lot more to a successful marriage than a heady rush of emotion. "A level head will carry a match much farther than a case of hormones can," she'd said.

And they certainly both could gain from this alliance. Through Synnamon, Conner would get Sherwood Cosmetics—signed, sealed and delivered. Through Conner, Synnamon would gain independence and perhaps even some value in Silas Sherwood's eyes. She wouldn't simply be his awkward daughter anymore.

It had started out all right, she supposed, and if it hadn't been for Silas's death, they might have rubbed along reasonably well together for years. Lots of married couples didn't have a great deal to say to each other. Her parents had certainly never talked much, so why should she and Conner be different?

They didn't fight, and they weren't incompatible in bed. She might not even have noticed how rarely Conner came to her room. They weren't living in a soap opera, after all—they were ordinary people.

But when Silas died, everything slowly began to come clear. It seemed to Synnamon that she'd been living in a frosted bubble for more years than she could count, but on the day of her father's funeral the fog had begun to dissipate. And she didn't like what she saw.

Things had come to a head a few weeks later, when Conner had come home one night and suggested that perhaps they should take a week off and get away, since people were starting to comment about how tired they both looked.

"No, thanks. Who cares what people think?" Synnamon had looked straight at him and added calmly, "We don't have to pretend any more, you know. In fact, I've been thinking that it would be best for both of us if we called a halt to this farce. You have what you wanted, Conner, and you don't need to worry about losing Sherwood. You're welcome to it. All I want is peace and quiet."

He had said, finally, that perhaps she was right, and he'd moved out the next day.

It had been the best thing for both of them, Synnamon knew. It was at least the honest thing. That was what she'd planned to tell the Contessa.

And as for her hopes of a family... Well, she'd survive without a child. Perhaps she'd adopt someday, or perhaps...

Suddenly there was a brassy taste in her mouth. Synnamon looked at the wreckage of her thumbnail. She'd unconsciously chewed off all the polish.

She wished she could convince herself that accounted for the chemical flavor on her tongue, but she knew better. That nasty taste had an entirely different source. Its origin wasn't oral at all, but mental—born of shock.

Now everything suddenly made sense. Her lack of appetite, the way the Pinnacle's motion had affected her, the virus that came and went, the sudden unbearable tiredness.

She'd have to go to work early in the morning and stop in the employees' shop for a quick manicure and a set of replacement nails. That way only the manicurist would suspect how nervous Synnamon was—and even she would have no way to know the reason behind that uneasiness.

But even before that, she'd have to run another errand. She'd stop by the nearest pharmacy for one of those home-testing kits. And as soon as she was alone, she'd find out for certain whether she was pregnant.

CHAPTER THREE

AND if she was…

It wouldn't change anything, Synnamon reminded herself. She was perfectly capable of raising a child. She had the financial resources, and now, with her job almost finished, she would have all the time in the world. She could take on the responsibility of a baby. *All* the responsibility of a baby.

She might as well be talking about the weight of the universe.

But there was a good chance she was only imagining things, she told herself firmly. It wasn't as if she had any real knowledge of what morning sickness felt like. And wasn't every woman different, anyway? Maybe her upset stomach was only a combination of a kooky virus and a mind made suggestible by a bad case of loneliness.

And the suspicion that she might be pregnant wasn't exactly a logical one, either. She and Conner had lived together for eight months, so perhaps it was foolish to think that on one single, desperate night they might have created a new life.

It wasn't impossible, of course—but it was improbable. Incredible. So unlikely that she was certainly not going to drive herself crazy by worrying about it.

But she wished it wasn't Christmas, and that she didn't have to wait till tomorrow for a pharmacy to open, so she could know for sure.

Synnamon's newly manicured hands shook as she locked herself into the half-bath off her office and ripped open

45

the home-testing kit. The instructions seemed a mile long, and she had trouble concentrating. But eventually she had followed all the directions, and she held her breath as she waited for the results.

She was quite certain what she wanted the answer to be, she told herself. The last thing she needed to complicate her life right now was a child. And yet...

The test strip slowly, inexorably, turned pink.

She stared at it, stunned by the evidence that she would not be spending next Christmas alone after all—for by then her baby would be four months old.

She bit her lip hard and sat down on the tiled counter next to the sink, still holding the test strip. What a tiny thing it was to change a life!

Two lives—hers, and that of the child she carried.

Panic threatened to overwhelm her. It was one thing to consider solitary child-raising in the abstract, but it was a bit different to contemplate a real-life, breathing, screaming baby.

Annie tapped on the bathroom door. ''Mrs. Welles? Are you all right?''

Synnamon had to swallow hard before she could answer. ''I'm fine, Annie. Be right out.''

Her hands were still shaking as she hurriedly gathered up all the paraphernalia and dumped it into the Tyler-Royale shopping bag in which she'd smuggled the kit into the building. She shoved the bag into the cabinet under the sink and said, as she came out, ''I've got just a little upset stomach—I think I celebrated a bit too much yesterday.''

Only then did she see who else was waiting for her. Conner was leaning against her desk with his arms folded across his chest, the long fingers of his left hand drumming gently against the sleeve of his deep charcoal suit.

"Mr. Welles is here," Annie said unnecessarily.

Conner, Synnamon thought desperately. How on earth was she going to break the news to Conner that in a well-meaning act of consolation he'd fathered her child?

What, she thought half-hysterically, would the Contessa advise? No matter how thorny the situation, the queen of etiquette had always had an answer. But what would she say about this tangle?

"Sorry to rush in on you," Conner said briskly, "especially at this hour of the morning. But I'm on my way to Fargo because there's been a contamination in one of the production lines at the plant up there."

"Contamination? What—"

"Nobody knows yet how it happened. I just wanted to let you know that you're apt to be getting some questions from customers when the rumors start to fly. As soon as I know what's going on I'll give you a call, and you can put out a statement. But in the meantime if you can just try to keep a lid on the speculation…"

Synnamon nodded, and her heartbeat steadied a little. "I'll take care of it, Conner."

"Of course you will." There was obviously no doubt in his mind. Synnamon supposed she should consider it a compliment.

Conner turned toward the door and then swung back abruptly to face her. "Are you all right, Synnamon? Really?"

Half of her wanted to blurt out her news right there and have it over and done with. But with Annie in the room, and Conner obviously anxious to be gone, it would hardly be fair to drop a bombshell like that.

Besides, she wanted a little time herself to come to

terms with this complication before she let the rest of the world in on it. She *needed* a little time. Surely it wasn't cowardly to want to think it over first?

"I'm fine," she said steadily.

Conner's smile didn't quite reach his eyes, Synnamon noticed. But then she suspected hers didn't, either.

"And pigs fly, too." He nodded toward her hands. "Biting your thumb now and then is one thing, but when you're wearing a full set of fake nails, Synnamon, it's a dead giveaway."

She raised one hand and stared at the offending fingertips. The acrylic nails looked just fine to her—perfectly natural and elegantly shaped. She'd have said this new product was by far the best adhesive nails Sherwood had ever produced. They were even lightweight and comfortable. But if Conner could tell at a glance...

She said wryly, "Maybe the real question you should be asking is how to improve the nails so they don't look fake."

"Oh, they wouldn't to most people," Conner assured her. "I'm just particularly attuned."

To the nails? Synnamon thought in sudden panic. *Or to me*?

"Don't forget I supervised the last research trials on that brand," he went on. "I'd recognize them a mile away."

She started to breathe again.

"If the problem is that you're already missing your job, Synnamon, I'm sure we can work something out."

"I'll certainly keep that in mind," she said dryly. "Don't let me make you miss your plane."

After he was gone, Annie said, "I'll start working up a standard answer for any questions, if you'd like."

Synnamon nodded. "Good idea."

Annie's voice was hesitant. ''Mr. Welles is right, you know. If you should change your mind and decide to stay—well, I just want you to know I completely understand.''

''Don't worry about it. It's not going to happen.'' Synnamon swallowed hard and sat in the overstuffed chair next to her desk. ''In fact, you may be handling the job even earlier than you expected, Annie. I don't think I'm fine, after all.''

She didn't want to tell him.

There's no reason to, a little voice at the back of her brain argued. It wasn't as if this incident would make a difference in the course of Conner's life. The responsibility was entirely hers. She was the one who'd invited this disaster, and she was the one who would have to deal with the consequences.

The divorce might not be quite final, but the marriage was long over—and that meant the days of expecting loyalty whether in sickness or in health were already past.

If she'd walked out in front of a truck and been injured, she wouldn't expect Conner to come running to her assistance. Well, this accident wasn't his fault, either, so why make a point of bringing him into it?

Because it's different, she told herself wearily. She couldn't keep a pregnancy hidden forever.

Or could she? If she finished her work and announced that she was moving away...

There was nothing keeping her in Denver. It was quite logical, with all the stress and changes in her life this year, that she'd want to start over somewhere else. She could sell the apartment and go to live in Phoenix for a while—in the Contessa's town house—while she made up her mind.

Except for one minor detail, she recalled. She'd promised to give Annie ninety days of support and training,
and she could hardly do that over the telephone.

No, she'd have to tell Conner. It was only fair to do
so, anyway. She'd simply have to be careful how she did
it, to make it clear that she didn't expect anything from
him.

Annie tapped on her office door. "Mr. Welles is on the
phone. Are you enough better to talk to him?"

"Of course." Synnamon glanced at her watch. Conner
had been in Fargo for just a few hours. She pushed the
damp washcloth off her forehead and sat up straight. After
spending most of the day in the chair, she was a bit light-
headed.

Annie looked concerned. "Shall I bring another cool
cloth?"

Synnamon stood and had to reach for the corner of her
desk to steady herself. "Not just now." She took a deep
breath and reached for the telephone. "Conner?"

"There's good news and bad news," he said. "The
contamination is bacterial."

And therefore it would be particularly nasty to combat,
Synnamon deduced.

"But we think we've already found the source, and if
that's confirmed, we can steam-clean the whole production line and start it up again. By the end of the week
everything could be back to normal."

She was jotting notes. "And there's enough product in
the warehouses to take care of demand in the meantime,
right?"

"Yes—except we'll have to test every batch in order
to be certain the contamination didn't sneak in earlier than
we think."

"All right. I'll tell everyone that there may be minor

delays in shipment because we're taking no chances with customer safety.''

''That's good. I'm going to stay here till it's all cleaned up, just to be certain.''

''That will look reassuring to some of our customers and suspicious to the rest, Conner.''

He laughed. ''Use your best judgment on who to tell.''

Synnamon was startled by the genuine amusement in his voice. She hadn't realized how long it had been since she'd heard anything of the sort.

He sobered. ''Are you feeling better?''

''Some. Conner—''

The word was out before she could stop herself, but immediately Synnamon thought better of it. To tell him like this, when he was two states away, would truly be the coward's way out. Not that she was looking forward to telling him face-to-face, either—but she needed to be able to see him when he heard the news. Only then could she judge his reaction and respond appropriately, by re-assuring him that she didn't blame him at all and that she didn't expect him to be bound by this mistake.

''I'm fine,'' she said. ''I think I just got some bad pâté at the deli. But everything's smooth here.''

She put down the telephone and dropped her face into her hands. Phoenix and the Contessa's town house looked more inviting than ever.

With the mess in Fargo finally under control, Conner was due back in Denver in the afternoon of New Year's Eve.

Synnamon couldn't make up her mind whether she wanted him to come to the office or stay away till after the holiday. She was pleased to have the production prob-lem solved, of course. She'd spent most of the week on the telephone, soothing nervous corporate accounts. But the closer she came to the time when she would have to confess her secret to Conner, the more jittery she grew.

At least physically she was feeling better. The morning sickness still came and went, but at least—unlike the day after Christmas—it no longer persisted around the clock or kept her from working.

The weather on the final day of December was almost as gloomy as Synnamon felt. The sky was so heavy and dark it was hard to tell where the clouds ended and the mountains began. If she was lucky, she thought, the predicted snow would materialize and the airport would close, stranding Conner in Fargo for the holiday.

As each hour ticked by and she did a few more things for the last time, Synnamon's sadness grew. From now on, when she spent time in the office it would be as Annie's assistant and adviser. This would no longer be her private retreat.

She had spent three full years within the four walls of this room—at least the most meaningful part of each day had found her there—and it wasn't going to be easy to give it up.

She'd had to fight for the opportunity to make a place for herself at Sherwood. It would have been far easier to go to work somewhere else, but deep inside, Synnamon had known that only if she could prove herself at Sherwood Cosmetics—in the family business—would she really believe in her own worth. And if along the way she could prove a thing or two to her father—well, that would be the icing on the gingerbread.

That was why, on the day after she'd graduated from college, she'd appeared in the waiting room outside her father's office, determined to sit there until Silas gave her a chance. Eventually, he'd grown tired of her persistence, and he'd assigned her a job.

Customer service wouldn't have been Synnamon's first choice, for she felt that her talent lay in juggling numbers, not people. But she'd been in no position to quibble. In fact, Synnamon had always thought Silas had sent her to customer service because he believed she'd soon be so discouraged and stressed by handling questions and complaints that she'd quit altogether. But then, Silas Sherwood had never known his daughter very well.

The first year had been especially tough, as she felt her way like a blind man through a mine field. Many of Sherwood's clients had been reluctant to deal with her, convinced she was a dilettante daughter with a manufactured job. She'd worked ferociously to develop relationships with the clients, to carve out enough authority so she could actually handle their problems, to figure out when to be sympathetic and when to be assertive.

Assertiveness still didn't come naturally to her. The difficulty of her own struggle was one of the reasons she'd agreed to help Annie with her adjustment. If there was one thing Synnamon fully understood, it was the feeling of being inadequate for the job.

Perhaps that was why, with Silas gone, the whole thing no longer seemed to matter. Though she felt sadness at the idea of leaving Sherwood and fear of the great unknowns that awaited her after she left the only job she'd ever held, there was also relief. She'd made a success of a difficult assignment and she no longer had anything to prove.

Now she just had to pack up the trivia of her life.

Synnamon picked up the silver-framed photograph of her mother from the credenza behind her desk and looked thoughtfully at the young, beautiful face of Rita Sherwood. By the time Synnamon had been old enough to recognize her mother's beauty, it had been overlaid with a veneer of hardness. The bitter dregs of unhappiness had taken the lively glow out of Rita's eyes and thinned the sensual lips to the sharp line Synnamon remembered.

She understood now that Silas had been no happier than his wife. Theirs had been a marriage that would have been better dissolved, but Rita's religious beliefs had not allowed divorce. So they had stayed together—not through thick and thin, Synnamon had heard her mother tell a friend once in an acid moment, but through thin, thinner and thinnest.

Only now did Synnamon really understand what Rita had meant, and she thanked heaven that she and Conner had had the good sense to see what lay ahead and get out before the unhappiness marred them both for life, while they could still break up without battling. At least, she thought, they had the advantage of being civilized about it. They were splitting decently, without recriminations or resentment or hard feelings, without argument or sharp words or fights over bits of property. In short, theirs was the perfect divorce.

Synnamon wrapped the frame in tissue paper and reached for the small Russian lacquer box that had stood next to the photograph. There were a thousand of her possessions in the office. She'd be the rest of the day packing them all up. She hadn't realized how many of her personal things had crept into her work space—almost more, she thought, than her apartment held.

Annie punched the button that turned off the speakerphone on Synnamon's desk and swiveled her chair. "How did that sound?"

"You did just fine," Synnamon said, and tried to soothe her conscience. It was only a tiny white lie, after all, to imply that she'd been listening intently to every word of the conversation. It wasn't the end of the world to have let her mind wander. If Annie had stumbled, she'd have heard.

"Thanks. You don't know what that means to me—knowing that you're there to back me up. Don't worry about packing everything today. There will be plenty of time later."

"But as of Monday morning it will be your office. And you'll want your own things around."

"Actually, I think I'd find it more comforting to have some of yours for a while." Annie's smile was wry. "That way I can pretend I'm only using your office temporarily while Sandra borrows mine. Do you think she's going to work out?"

"She has potential," Synnamon said carefully. "But be careful to treat her as an employee, not a friend. Especially until you have a little more experience as a boss, it's better for everyone not to get the two things confused."

Annie sighed. "I know. There's so much to remember, and it's so easy to slip up."

"You'll get the hang of it. It just takes practice, and getting in the habit of thinking before you start talking." Synnamon looked around. "I thought I had another box somewhere."

"No—that was the last of them. There's a shopping bag in the bathroom, though. I just noticed it this morning." Annie bounced out of her chair and went after it.

Synnamon's eyes widened in shock. How could she have forgotten to dispose of that damned bag and its telltale contents? But she knew how it had happened. Between juggling phone calls all week and feeling ill at the least convenient moments, she'd put the test kit out of her mind. Besides, she admitted, she'd *wanted* to forget the whole thing—to pretend that it wasn't real.

Annie was back in a moment, brandishing Synnamon's Tyler-Royale bag. "I thought it was empty, but there's something—" She dumped the bag's contents onto the desk blotter.

Synnamon knew the instant the brand name emblazoned on the box registered in Annie's mind. The woman had two small children herself. There was no doubt she'd recognize a kit for a home pregnancy test when she saw one.

"Oh, my," Annie murmured. "I had no idea."

Synnamon braced herself. Would the reaction be delight? Congratulations? Shock? And did this mean she'd better rush to tell Conner, before the grapevine got hold of the news? She didn't question Annie's discretion—but if Annie had spotted that bag, the janitorial staff might have, too.

Annie's face was absolutely expressionless. She didn't even look at Synnamon. "I noticed when I came back from lunch," she said, "that Mr. Welles is in the building now."

She sounded as calm, Synnamon thought, as if she was really changing the subject. Which of course they both knew she wasn't...not really.

Synnamon's heart was thumping. She hadn't expected him back quite this early.

Of course, she didn't have to rush down to his office right this minute. She could wait till next week to tell him, and at least keep Sherwood Cosmetics out of it.

Right, she told herself dryly. *It'll make everything so much easier if I just phone him up on Monday and ask him to lunch. And over the hors d'oeuvres I'll just casually mention that we're having a baby!*

"If you can take care of the rest of those calls,"

Synnamon said, sounding much calmer than she felt, "I'll go and check in with Mr. Welles."

There would never be a good time to tell him, she reminded herself as she walked down the hall. She'd have to be careful how she handled it, of course—but no matter what his reaction, at least that much of the difficulty would be behind her.

But Conner couldn't see her. "He's tied up," Carol said, "and I don't even have a good idea when he'll be free. I'll call your office, if you like, as soon as he can fit you in." She must have seen the strain in Synnamon's face, for she added gently, "I'm sorry."

"That's fine," Synnamon said. "I'll catch him later."

She supposed she should have expected it. After a week away, Conner's in-basket was probably brimming with problems to handle and calls to return. That was exactly the reason she'd made the rule for herself to always phone for an appointment before going to his office. It was a rule she had broken today without even remembering it.

She had worked up her nerve for nothing, and now she felt as if there was a rock lodged in her throat—a dry, crumbly, dusty piece of limestone that was likely to stay there until the deed was done.

She didn't want to face Annie just yet, so she wandered down to the staff dining room, got a bottle of orange juice and sat down to drink it. A caterer's crew was working in the kitchen, putting the final touches on the office New Year's party. The bustle made her nervous, and with the half-full bottle in her hand she started toward her office.

As she passed the executive suite, the door of Conner's office swung open, and she caught just a glimpse of him. She knew he couldn't see her, standing in the hallway outside the waiting room, but the rock in her throat suddenly felt even larger. He seemed taller—or was it just

her fear of facing him that made him seem more impos-
ing?

She heard him laugh, and then she saw the redhead who
was standing beside him with her hand placed confidingly
on the sleeve of his jacket. The rock suddenly grew into
a boulder, almost choking off her air supply.

"I'll talk to you later, Nick," he said. "Think it over,
and let me know."

Nick. The name seemed to echo in Synnamon's head,
but why should it sound familiar?

Finally she recalled his telephone conversation on the
day she'd gone to tell him about the Contessa. Hadn't he
been talking to a Nick that day? It had been a business
conversation, Synnamon was sure, and she'd assumed it
was a man he was talking to—but it might have been this
woman instead. She could be a supplier, a customer, an
ad agency representative...any number of things.

What was it Morea had said about Conner seeing someone? That she'd heard things, that was it. *Maybe*, Synnamon thought, *I should have asked her exactly what it
was she'd heard.*

On the other hand, she reminded herself, there was no
point in acting like an idiot. It wasn't as if she had any
rights where Conner was concerned, or even any real interest.

But she couldn't help noticing that he looked more
alive, somehow, right now—with the redhead's hand on
his sleeve—than Synnamon remembered seeing him in
months.

Before she could move, he'd closed the office door
once more, and the redhead came across the waiting room.
As if she had radar, her gaze focused on Synnamon.

Almost as if she recognizes me, Synnamon thought. It
made sense, of course, that a woman who was interested

in Conner would have an idea of what his wife looked like and be curious about her. Conner might even have described her.

Now there's a comforting thought, she told herself wryly.

She gave the redhead a cool, polite nod—the same as she would to any stranger she met in the halls—and went to her office.

The shopping bag had disappeared, but Annie had come up with another box and was carefully packing the things Synnamon had already wrapped in tissue. "Carol called just a minute ago," she said, "to say Mr. Welles was free now. But I didn't know where you were, so—"

"It doesn't matter, Annie." Synnamon's lips felt stiff. "It's not important any more. In fact, I think I'll just go on home, since there's really nothing left for me to do here."

Annie sounded shocked. "And miss the party? But—"

"I'm not much in the mood for a party." Synnamon forced herself to smile. "I wouldn't want to keep everyone else from having fun by being a grump."

"But you can't! I mean, you're never a grump, and besides..." Annie drew a deep breath. "Carol will kill me for telling you this, I suppose. But you see, Mrs. Welles, it's not just a New Year's Eve celebration, it's going to be a farewell party for you."

Synnamon's heart sank. It was one thing to skip an ordinary office party, something else to miss one given in her honor. The questions her absence would raise didn't bear thinking about. She was stuck.

"That's very thoughtful," she managed to say. The Contessa, she thought, would have been proud of how calm she sounded.

She stayed in her office as long as she conscientiously

could, and by the time she arrived the party was already
in full swing. Synnamon asked the bartender for ginger
ale in a champagne flute, and she was just turning away
from the bar when Conner—with the redhead beside
him—came up and asked for two Scotches with water.

How cozy, Synnamon thought, that they liked the same
drink. But what in heaven's name was the redhead doing
there in the first place? She had to bite her tongue to keep
from asking Conner just when he'd decided to open Sherwood parties to dates as well as employees.

"Synnamon," he said, "I'd like you to meet Nicole
Fox. Nick helped sort out the problems in Fargo."

Fargo, Synnamon thought woodenly. Conner had
sounded happy when he was in Fargo. She remembered
thinking that she hadn't heard that note in his voice in
months. Was this woman the reason?

"Is that where you're from, Nicole?" she asked, politely holding out a hand.

"No, I'm based here in Denver." Nicole's handshake
was warm and firm. "Conner and I are old friends." She
smiled at him.

A meaningful smile, Synnamon thought. One that contained all sorts of hidden messages.

"When he called to ask my opinion of the contamination, I happened to be free," Nicole went on, without
taking her eyes off Conner's face. "So I flew up."

"Nick was a tremendous help." Conner handed Nicole
her cocktail glass and raised his own in a casual salute.
"In fact, I've offered her the position as head of research
and development."

Synnamon was stunned.

Think it over and let me know, Conner had told the
woman at his office door just a couple of hours ago. Obviously this was what they'd been discussing.

She told herself it could be worse. She just didn't quite, at the moment, see how.

She swallowed hard and made some feeble comment. Conner's eyebrows went up, but before he could comment Annie called Synnamon over to present a gift from all the employees.

It's none of your business who he hires, she tried to tell herself as the party wore on. But the truth was that, however much she'd like to deny it, she was still involved. Even though she was no longer formally employed by Sherwood Cosmetics, she was still a stockholder, and she would always feel a responsibility to her father's employees. And this, she knew in her heart, was a very bad decision for everyone.

She couldn't square it with her conscience not to bring her objections to Conner's attention before it was too late for him to change his mind. Whether it would do any good was another question entirely, but she had to try.

But by the time she was free, Conner was nowhere to be found. She sought out Carol, who said, "I wouldn't be surprised if he was going to do a little more work. You might try his office."

The wing of the building that held the executive offices was hushed and only dimly lighted. Synnamon hesitated outside Conner's closed door. What if he wasn't alone? She hadn't seen Nicole at the party in the last half hour, either, and if they'd retreated to his office together…

Until this moment, Synnamon had almost forgotten the rumor that one of the couches in Silas's office unfolded into a bed. She'd heard the whispers in her first months at Sherwood, but the talk had always been quickly suppressed when she appeared, and she'd never known if there was any truth to the story. She wouldn't have been surprised to know of a mistress—in fact, she'd have been far more amazed if Silas had continued to be faithful to his marriage vows through the long and miserable years. But somehow a fold-out bed in his office didn't seem quite like Silas. A cozy little penthouse at the Brown Palace, on the other hand…

But if there *had* been a bed in the office, it was still there, since Conner hadn't changed the furniture. And the suite was awfully quiet.

Synnamon knocked, but there was no answer. Almost as an afterthought, she turned the knob and was surprised when the door opened. The office was dark, however, and obviously deserted.

She started to back out, but suddenly nausea overtook her and she rushed toward Conner's bathroom instead.

She was over the worst when the bathroom lights snapped on. She put up a hand in self-defense against the blinding glare, and Conner said, "Somebody should have warned you that punch Carol makes will get you every time."

"I didn't even try the punch."

"Oh, that's right. You were drinking champagne. To what do I owe this honor? It isn't even the closest bathroom."

Synnamon pulled herself to her feet, ignoring the hand he offered, and reminded herself that much as she'd like to take a swing at him it wouldn't get her anywhere. And telling him about the baby wouldn't be a great idea at the moment, either. She had a real and solid reason to have sought him out, and it would be foolish to let herself be distracted—no matter how annoying he was.

"I'm not trying to interfere, Conner, but…" She paused and patted a tissue across her temple. "Do you mind if I sit down?"

"Oh, please do." He led the way into the office and

snapped on the lights. "Carol said you were anxious to talk to me this afternoon, but then you changed your mind. Have you changed it back again?"

Synnamon glanced from the couch to the love seat. Which one of them would be most likely to hold a mattress, tucked away from casual sight? *I don't care*, she reminded herself.

"Believe me," Conner said, "I'm delighted to know you don't intend to interfere. So what did you want to talk to me about?"

Synnamon smothered a sigh at the faint irony in his voice. "Nicole Fox. I don't think you should make her head of research and development." She sat on the love seat.

"Oh? It was your idea, after all." Conner perched on the arm of the couch.

"Mine?" Her voice was little more than a squeak.

"Yes. You're the one who suggested we bring in new blood, all that sort of thing."

"Well, I didn't suggest it be hers!"

Conner's eyebrows soared.

Oh, great, she thought. *Now I sound jealous!* "I don't have any idea what her qualifications are—"

"That's right. You don't."

"But it doesn't matter. Naming her—or any other woman—to that job would be a big mistake."

"I'm listening."

Synnamon took a deep breath. She had one chance, and she'd better make it good. "Putting a woman in charge of those right-wing men would be asking for disaster. I don't have anything against Nicole Fox, in particular—"

"I'll certainly keep that in mind, Synnamon."

"In other words," she said tartly, "you've already decided."

How long had he had this move in mind? Conner hadn't really said, when Anderson made his announcement last week, that he was going to offer the position to one of the current people. Had he planned even then to hire Nicole Fox?

"What else?" Conner asked.

Synnamon was taken aback. "What do you mean, what else?"

"What else is bothering you? You've obviously had something on your mind since this afternoon, and it can't have been Nick, because you didn't know about her till the party. And since you don't seem to be drunk after all..."

If she'd been feeling better, Synnamon might have kept her head. But she was far too irritated to think before she spoke. "Oh, it's nothing much," she snapped. "I'm just pregnant, that's all."

He drew in a short, harsh breath, and wary silence descended on the room. Synnamon could hear her own heartbeat throbbing unsteadily.

Instantly, she regretted letting her temper get the best of her. What had happened to her resolve to be decent, amicable, civilized—no matter what? Breaking the news to him so harshly was no way to get along.

"I'm sorry, Conner," she said quietly. "I had no idea that little encounter in Phoenix would end up in such a mess."

He was so still that she wondered for a moment if he'd even heard her.

"It's nothing for you to worry about," she offered finally. "I'll deal with it."

"You'll *deal* with it how? An abortion?" He sounded perfectly calm, as if—once the moment of shock had passed—he'd had no trouble at all reaching a decision.

Synnamon was stunned. Did he honestly think she was capable of destroying a life? Even though she didn't want this child any more than he did...

No, she realized, that wasn't quite the case. It was the pregnancy she didn't particularly want to deal with, and the complications it represented—complications like Conner's attitude. But as for the *child*...

Something she'd never felt before surged through her body—a combination of heat and emotion that threatened to engulf her. Was this, she wondered almost in awe, what it felt like to be a mother? This almost overpowering desire to protect—at any cost—the tiny helpless being inside her?

Thank heaven, she thought, it was really none of Conner's business what she did. She certainly didn't need to convince him, or even let herself be drawn into an argument about it.

"Well, it is the perfect answer, don't you think?" Synnamon said, with a calm that matched his own. She pushed herself to her feet. "Sorry if I've upset your evening, Conner—I probably shouldn't have bothered you with it at all." She managed a note of solicitousness. "You won't lie awake tonight worrying about it, will you?"

She didn't wait for an answer, though. She was out the door before he moved and home before she stopped shaking. She paced the floor in her living room, muttering, cursing him. How *dare* he accuse her of wanting to destroy a child?

Eventually, however, she calmed enough to see that however unflattering his attitude, there were certain advantages for her. Perhaps it was just as well Conner felt that way. There would be no question of him wanting to be involved, and her life would be a great deal simpler because of his detachment. She could bring up her child in peace, without having to deal with a reluctant, part-time second parent. There wouldn't be any quarrels over schools or methods of discipline, over visitation rights or child support, or even whether the kid should have hockey skates or dancing shoes. Yes, they would be better off this way, all three of them.

Eventually, she started to feel calmer, and after a while she even began to see things from Conner's point of view. Not about the abortion, of course—there was no under-standing that. But she could appreciate his shock—heaven knew she'd felt that herself. She could comprehend the consternation he'd felt, the instant panic over what she might demand from him.

His reaction was partly her fault, anyway, Synnamon admitted. She could have broken the news a great deal more smoothly than she had. She could have reassured him, made it clear that she was telling him only out of a desire for fairness, not because she expected—or wanted—anything from him.

Instead, she'd dumped the facts on him like a load of gold bars. No wonder the man had been stunned. He might even have thought for a moment that she was going to suggest they resume their marriage.

In the silence of the apartment, the click of a key in the front door lock seemed to echo like a gunshot. Syn-namon swung around and stared through the small foyer just as one of the double doors swung open.

Conner was standing there, his trench coat draped over his arm, pulling his key from the lock.

She hadn't thought to ask him to return his key. She hadn't even considered changing the locks after he'd moved out. She'd never felt physically unsafe with him, and it wasn't the sort of divorce where one of them would hide assets or make off with personal property in a desire for revenge.

"What are you doing here at this hour?" she managed.

One dark eyebrow tilted and he said evenly, "I couldn't make it any earlier, I'm afraid. I had a few things to finish up before I could leave."

"That's not what I—"

He closed the door with a firm little click. "I must say it's very thoughtful of you to have waited up, Synnamon, so we could take up our discussion where you so rudely broke it off."

CHAPTER FOUR

SYNNAMON had trouble finding her voice. "*I* was rude? And what, exactly, were you?" She realized that approach was likely to end in nothing but petty squabbling, so she took a deep breath and tried again. "I don't think we have anything at all to discuss. I'm sorry I bothered you with this, Conner. It's not your problem, after all—"

Conner shook his trench coat out with a snap and hung it in the hall closet. "It certainly sounds like a problem to me."

"It's a complication, yes. But it has nothing to do with you," Synnamon said stubbornly.

"Because you're going to end the pregnancy." It was not a question.

"And you're obviously worried about it. Why, Conner? Are you afraid I won't go through with it?" The tremor in her voice was a far cry from the bravado she was trying for. "Well, whether I do or not, it still isn't any of your concern." She raised her head proudly. "I lied, you know. I was trying to shake you up."

"You succeeded," he said dryly. "Are you going to tell me now that you're not pregnant after all?"

Synnamon wasn't listening. "This isn't your baby. It has nothing to do with what happened in Phoenix. I don't know why I told you that. Desperation, probably. But—"

He actually smiled, but there was no matching sparkle in his eyes. "Oh, no. It's a little late to try that approach." He took two steps toward her, and despite her resolve to stand her ground, Synnamon backed away from him and

68

collided with the edge of the French door between the foyer and the living room. Only half-conscious of the bump, she rubbed her arm and stared uncertainly at him.

"If I had any reason to believe you wanted me back," Conner went on thoughtfully, "I might be convinced you'd made up a story about being pregnant, or conveniently assumed I was the father of a child who might actually be someone else's. But the fact is, you don't have any reason to lie about the baby being mine, because you *don't* want me back."

He stripped off his suit jacket and draped it over the back of the nearest chair.

He might as well be planting a flag of conquest, Synnamon thought bitterly.

"So I'm afraid there's only one logical conclusion," Conner went on inexorably, "and that's to believe you told the truth the first time around—that you *are* pregnant, and it *is* my baby. Now, shall we cut out the nonsense and get down to business?"

Synnamon bit her lip. "If you want to be technical," she conceded, "you've got it right. But I was the one who was careless, and I'll deal with the consequences. All the consequences."

The silence seemed a living thing. The air positively sizzled. Why, Synnamon wondered, hadn't her declaration eased the tension as she'd intended it should? Her knees were shaking, and she had to lean against the French door to keep herself upright.

Conner's forehead wrinkled. "You shouldn't be standing." He stepped forward, a hand outstretched. "In fact, you should be in bed."

"I would have been, if you hadn't turned up," Synnamon pointed out. She pushed herself away from the door. "Look, Conner, why don't you just go away and forget I said anything?"

"And leave the loose ends to you."

Perhaps she shouldn't have been so annoyed at the idea that to him the baby was no more than a loose end, a minor annoyance to be destroyed with as little thought as he'd clip a dangling thread. She tried to remind herself that the less interested he was in the child as a person, the less trouble she'd face in the long run. But why couldn't she seem to convince Conner that she didn't want anything from him?

Strain and exhaustion and the aftermath of nausea combined to make her head spin, and suddenly she was just too tired to argue any more. Why should it matter what he thought, anyway? Conner's opinion wasn't going to change her plans.

"Leave your key on the hall table," she ordered. "And lock the door behind you."

Synnamon kept a hand on the wall to steady herself as she walked down the hallway to the master bedroom. She didn't look over her shoulder, but she knew he had followed her as far as the foyer and that he stood there watching until she reached her bedroom and firmly closed the door.

Her sleep was restless, at best, and Synnamon woke to a gray Denver day with a headache to match. What a way to start out a new year, she thought, and considered pulling the pillow over her head and staying in bed.

But she wasn't likely to be able to sleep. Her mind was running in circles, and her stomach was churning. Some food might help, unappetizing as the idea of eating was at the moment. Coffee, on the other hand, was positively inviting.

The longing for caffeine pushed her upright. She

shoved her feet into the most comfortable old slippers she owned, wrapped herself in a terry robe and started for the kitchen.

It was only her imagination, of course, that made Synnamon think she could smell coffee. Mrs. Ogden had taken the holiday off. But the imaginary scent reminded her of the earliest days of her marriage, when Conner had occasionally brought her coffee in bed. She told herself sternly that she had better things to do than dwell on a few good, sentimental memories.

She was yawning as she walked into the kitchen, and for a moment, with her eyes squeezed almost shut, she didn't see him. When she did, Synnamon had to blink twice before she could focus.

Conner was standing at the range, the snow-white sleeves of his shirt rolled to the elbow, coating an omelet pan with melted butter. His hands were steady and his gaze was fixed firmly on his task. He looked up at her only briefly before turning to the bowl full of eggs next to the pan.

She stared at him. "I thought I told you to leave your key on the hall table," she said ominously.

"And I will. When I'm finished with it."

"Oh, you're finished, all right."

Conner shook his head. "We never completed our discussion. Besides, you didn't seem in the best condition to be alone last night, so I thought I'd better stay."

It was no longer his obligation to be concerned about her—but it was an odd mixture of annoyance and comfort that tumbled through her veins. Synnamon thrust her hands into the deep pockets of her terry robe. "Well, I hope you didn't have any trouble finding your way around!"

The barb seemed to bounce off him. "Not at all, thank

you.'' His voice was perfectly calm. ''I used the guest room so often in the last few months I lived here that I felt right at home.''

There was no answer to that, of course. Obviously, with her head aching, Synnamon was going to be no match for him this morning. At least she hadn't been dreaming the coffee. She moved past him and across the narrow kitchen to get a mug. ''There's no cream,'' she said, almost defiantly. ''I haven't kept it on hand since you left.''

''I noticed. I had the doorman bring some up.''

''Oh, that's great. Now the whole building will know.''

''That I spent the night? And why should anyone care? We are still married, you know. Would you care for toast?'' Efficiently, he buttered two slices and offered her one.

Synnamon took it. It was her loaf of bread, after all. He wasn't doing her any enormous favor to have dropped a slice in the toaster.

He bit into his own toast. ''Or have you been in the habit of entertaining overnight guests, and now the whole building is watching to see who's next?''

''Of course not.''

Conner smiled a little. ''I didn't think so.''

Too late, Synnamon wondered if she should have lied. Perhaps it still wasn't too late to persuade him that the baby wasn't his. *Dreamer*, she accused herself.

He tested the pan's temperature and stirred the eggs once more. His hands were perfectly steady as he poured the mixture into the sizzling butter. ''Besides, I asked the doorman if you'd been seeing anyone—and he said you hadn't.''

''You—'' Synnamon was almost speechless with fury. She took a deep breath, and then another, before she could control herself. ''All right, dammit,'' she said. ''Let's take this from the top. How many times do I have to tell you this baby is not your business?''

Conner reached for a spatula and lifted the very edge of the omelet to let the uncooked egg run underneath, against the hot pan. The motions were smooth and easy, as if he had nothing else on his mind. And yet there was a wariness in the set of his shoulders, in the way he held his head. ''About this abortion—''

Synnamon sighed. He'd know the truth soon enough, anyway. Maybe it would be better to sort everything out now. ''I'm not going to do that, Conner.''

''Then why did you say you were?''

''Because you made me furious by assuming that would be my first reaction.'' Synnamon sat at the breakfast bar, cradling her coffee mug between her hands. ''But no matter what you want, I can't do that.''

''Well, that's something.'' He cut the finished omelet into two pieces, slid half onto a plate and surrounded it with fresh buttered toast before setting it in front of her. Then he fixed the other half, filled his coffee cup and sat down with his plate. ''Why the hell did you think I was standing guard?''

''Because you *didn't* want me to?'' Her head was reeling. ''Oh, that's rich. As if I could run right down to the corner drug store on New Year's Eve... Well, I'm glad we got that settled. You can stop worrying about me destroying the baby, and I can get on with my life.''

''Not so fast. What *are* you going to do?''

''How many choices are there?'' Deliberately, she let irony drip from her voice. ''I'll keep the baby, of course. What else can I do?''

''And bring it up the way you were raised?''

There was something about his tone that made the hair

on the back of her neck stand on end. "What does that mean?"

Conner picked up a bit of toast and systematically shredded it. "There's more than one way to destroy a child, you know."

"Are you implying I'm incapable of being a decent mother?"

"Your upbringing wasn't your fault," he mused. "But if that's what you intend, this kid is going to be neurotic from the outset."

"Just like me, I suppose you mean?" Synnamon said icily.

"There's going to have to be some balance from somewhere."

"And I suppose you feel obligated to provide it? Look, Conner, it's downright decent of you to offer, but—"

"Thank you. You don't know what that does for my ego."

Synnamon ignored the interruption. "But I've told you and told you there's no need for you to be involved. It's only going to cause unnecessary complications if you insist on playing any part in this child's life. You're being shortsighted and completely unfair to yourself, to me *and* to the child—"

"If you want to get into a quarrel about unfairness, Synnamon, let me warn you—"

"No," she said quickly. "I don't want to quarrel about anything. I just want to get the rules hashed out right now, so nobody's confused about where we stand."

"I'm listening."

"You don't need to worry that I'll be calling you up to come to dance programs or piano recitals, so we can pretend to be a normal family." Her voice dripped irony.

"And I won't expect you to follow the rules on visitation times, either."

"That's perfectly all right with me. I don't find anything particularly inviting about taking over a kid for every other weekend and a month in the summer."

The level voice was almost frightening, Synnamon thought. Not only hadn't Conner reacted to her sarcasm, which surprised her, but he sounded as if he hadn't even heard it. As if he had a different agenda altogether.

"And I don't plan to baby-sit while you're out on a date, either," Conner went on easily. "So don't even think about asking."

"Don't worry, I won't." She took a deep breath. "So what are you suggesting instead? That you drop by once a year or so, when it's convenient for you? Look, Conner, if you want to do something nice for this child, why not make it easy on us all? I'm asking you one last time. Let's cut things off clean right now and pretend this never happened."

He looked at her levelly over the edge of his coffee mug. "I didn't say I wouldn't see the child regularly, Synnamon. I said I wouldn't be satisfied with the normal schedule for divorced parents."

Synnamon tried to tell herself she was furious, but she knew better. The ache deep inside her wasn't anger, it was pure fear. "Then what do you want?"

He crunched a bite of toast. "I want this child," he said simply. "And I will not settle for less."

Synnamon's heart felt as cold as the omelet that had congealed on the plate in front of her. She stared across the breakfast bar at him.

She didn't feel hurt, exactly, or even surprised. Her chest ached, she told herself, because she'd been idiot enough not to see what was really going on. She should have realized that Conner wouldn't turn his back on a child, no matter how unwanted or unplanned that baby was.

But this declaration was even more than that. He had matter-of-factly proclaimed that this child was his and his alone. It was just one more way he was like Silas Sherwood.

Her voice trembled. "If you're going to try to take the baby away from me—"

"It wouldn't be my first choice. Even an inadequate mother is better than none at all."

Relief flickered through her, to be drowned almost instantly by fury. He might as well have come straight out and said she was nothing more, in his eyes, than an incubator! "Then I really don't see what you mean."

"Don't you?" His voice was almost gentle. "You must not want to see, then—because you're certainly not stupid."

Synnamon could feel her heartbeat. It was an irregular, dull thud deep in her chest, and it hurt.

Conner picked up his empty plate and carried it to the dishwasher. Efficiently he loaded it and the omelet pan, filled the detergent cup and pushed the button to start the cycle.

As if, Synnamon thought, he'd been doing it all along. As if he thought he had the right.

Over the hiss of the water, he said, "Whatever had happened last night, Synnamon, I wouldn't have left. Because, you see, I'm here—in this apartment, and in your life—to stay."

The expression in his eyes, she thought, was almost sympathetic.

"In fact," he went on softly, "for want of a better word, you could say I've come home."

* * *

Synnamon sat at the breakfast bar long after Conner had left the kitchen. The irregular rush of water in the dishwasher mimicked the flow of blood through her body, sometimes surging with anger and adrenaline, sometimes slowing with fear and lassitude.

Home. The word rasped like sandpaper in her brain. It was bad enough that he'd come back at all, but to lightly announce that he was moving in and staying, that he'd come *home*—as if this had ever really been his home.

He couldn't get away with it, that was all. The first thing she'd do was call her attorney. Morea Landon, Synnamon was sure, wouldn't mince words about Conner's behavior.

She left her untouched plate on the breakfast bar and headed for her bedroom and the most private phone she could find. Beyond the open door of the hall bath, she heard an almost tuneless whistling and saw a neatly arranged array of brass and rubber pieces laid out on a spotless white towel at the edge of the sink.

Despite herself, she paused outside the door. "What are you doing to the faucet?" she accused.

"I'm stopping it from dripping. Are you objecting?"

She'd be a fool if she did, Synnamon knew, since she'd reported the leak twice already to the building superintendent. "How kind of you to make yourself useful," she said sweetly.

Conner didn't even look up. "I'm sure you'll find all sorts of ways I'll come in handy."

Why, Synnamon wondered, did she bother to bait him? It was a waste of time.

She dialed Morea's home number from memory and lay back against the satin bolster on her bed to wait for the call to go through. From the wall opposite, above a low chest where Synnamon stored her sweaters, the Con-

tessa watched her. A much younger Contessa, painted by
one of the most renowned artists of the day, wearing her
trademark strand of perfect pearls—the pearls she had
given Synnamon to wear on her wedding day.

What would the Contessa think of this mess?

Loss and loneliness engulfed Synnamon. What she
wouldn't give to be able to put her head down in the
Contessa's lap just once more and confess what an idiot
she'd been.

The telephone clicked, and Morea's breezy answering
machine message reminded Synnamon that her attorney
had said she was going skiing after Christmas. They were
going to Telluride, Morea had told her—and Synnamon
couldn't remember if she'd even mentioned when she'd
be home.

Synnamon put the phone down without leaving a message. She'd call Morea's law office tomorrow, and if she
wasn't back yet…

I can't last till tomorrow, she thought suddenly. The
longer Conner had to entrench himself, the more difficult
it would be to dislodge him. She'd better do something,
and fast, before he convinced himself that she'd invited
him to move in and supervise her life.

She found him in the small television room, flipping
channels on her tiny set. "Watching the parades?" she
asked.

Conner shook his head. "Waiting for the football game
to start."

"Good, I'm glad to know I'm not interrupting." She
perched on the edge of a chair. "Let's try this once more,
shall we?"

"Is there something left to say?"

"Surely you don't actually believe you can just move
in here like this."

His brow furrowed. "Why not? I've done it."

"We are not going to have any continuing relationship."

"Now that's where you're wrong. As long as we share a child, neither one of us can exactly pretend the other doesn't exist."

"All right," Synnamon admitted. "You've got a point there, but don't you see that the baby is a different thing altogether? We can't, personally…the two of us, I mean…" She was stammering.

"Live together? Why not?" He put the television remote control aside. "We intended to, when we married."

"Well, yes. But that's all over now."

"The important facts haven't changed at all, Synnamon. We didn't go into this marriage all dazed with romance and passion. We did what sensible people have done for hundreds of years—we chose, with our eyes wide open, to be partners. We married with the intention of building an alliance—and a family, if that was meant to be—that would last a lifetime."

She couldn't argue with the assessment of their marriage. It *had* been far more partnership than romantic passion. But the appraisal made her insides freeze nonetheless. She'd always known he'd been as attracted to Sherwood Cosmetics as to Synnamon—but had Conner really not found her even minimally appealing on a personal level?

"Then you changed your mind and wanted a divorce," Conner went on calmly, "and because that was a decision that affected only the two of us, I went along."

"Exactly," Synnamon agreed. *Now*, she thought, *we're getting somewhere*. "And we also, if you'll recall, made an agreement to be civilized about the whole divorce. We haven't gotten bogged down in fights over petty things yet, so surely there's no reason we can't settle this reasonably, too.''

''A child is not exactly a petty thing.''

Synnamon took a deep breath and tried to keep her tone reasonable. ''I didn't mean to imply it was. I was just trying to make clear that under the circumstances, I'm quite willing to take full responsibility for what happened. Since it really doesn't involve you, there's no reason to quarrel about it. We'd already agreed to an amicable divorce, so—''

''Of course, that was before we so *amicably* created a child.''

Synnamon was speechless. She was amazed he could enunciate so clearly when his jaw was set like concrete.

''If there had already been a child when you first asked for a divorce,'' Conner went on, ''I wouldn't have been so willing to go along. I would have reminded you of the bargain you'd struck, and I'd have held you to the contract between us.'' He settled a little deeper into his chair, as if staking a claim.

''Conner,'' she said desperately, ''you can't force someone to stay married.''

In the dim light of the television room his eyes had darkened to pure, passionate purple. ''Can you honestly tell me, Synnamon, that you love me any less today than you did on our wedding day?''

She gasped. ''That's not fair, Conner. Love never had anything to do with it.''

''Exactly. And everything else about our contract is still precisely the same, too. Except now there *is* a child—and so the divorce is off. You're my wife, Synnamon. And you're going to stay my wife.''

The flat calm of his voice was more convincing than any amount of shouting or arm-waving could have been.

He was dangerously gentle. In fact, she thought with a twinge of panic, he sounded as if he could afford to be compassionate—as if they were playing a life-size game of chess and only he could see the board.

There was no point in arguing with him, of course—or even answering. That would have to be Morea's job, she concluded. Synnamon had done everything she could do.

But neither, she decided, would she avoid him. It was her apartment, after all. *He* was the one who didn't belong, so why should she shut herself in her bedroom? Instead, she rummaged through a stack of magazines and curled up on the couch to read, with the subdued bustle of the pregame show as a background.

On a normal holiday, she couldn't help but think, she'd probably have brought a briefcase full of work home with her. There were always customer inquiries to answer, new-product data to read, problems to research—and the constant ringing of the telephone in her office made it difficult to concentrate there.

Now all that would be Annie's job, and Synnamon was reading magazines.

A roar from the television warned her that someone had scored a touchdown. Not Conner's team, she concluded, sneaking a quick look at him over the top of her magazine, since he was frowning.

Or was he thinking of other matters, and not the game at all? The man couldn't be happy at the turn his life had taken in the last twenty-four hours. Facing impending and less than welcome fatherhood created enough tension all by itself. Moving into the apartment and resuming the appearance of a marriage would be even worse…except, of course, that he wasn't actually going to do either of those things. Morea would put a stop to that soon enough.

She thought idly about what he'd said last night when

he first came into the apartment. *I had a few things to finish up*, wasn't that it? She wondered what those things had been. Had he, for instance, told Nicole Fox about the baby?

The very thought made her feel hollow. *With sympathy*, she told herself. Poor Nicole must have seen her future swept away by Conner's single careless act and his quixotic decision.

Of course, if she'd just be patient for awhile... Maybe, Synnamon thought, she should make it a point to talk to the woman.

"Hungry?" Conner asked.

Her thoughts had been so far away that she had to consider the question. "No."

"You can't live on coffee, you know."

She couldn't quite keep the tart edge out of her voice. "Don't you mean the baby can't?"

Conner shrugged. "Same thing." His gaze wandered to the action on the field.

She sniffed and buried her nose in her magazine. That was an unpleasant harbinger of things to come, she thought. If he was planning to be her shadow all through the pregnancy so she didn't damage *his* baby...

From a corner of her subconscious so deeply buried that she'd been unaware of its existence floated a hazy memory. Her mother had been ill one winter....

Rita Sherwood had just come home from the hospital, in fact, and Synnamon, who'd worried for days about her absent mother as only a four-year-old can, had slipped away from her baby-sitter to make sure Rita was all right. She was hovering on the landing when Silas came out of his study, and instead of running down into her mother's arms, she'd slipped into the shadows at the turn of the staircase.

The conversation she'd overheard hadn't meant anything to her then, and she could recall only the haziest of phrases. Silas had said something that sounded like *criminal carelessness*, and later he'd referred to *my son*.

Now the meaning was all too clear. By that time, Rita had obviously held value in her husband's eyes only for the son she might produce, and when her second pregnancy ended without Silas's longed-for heir, even that bit of worth had vanished like the morning mist.

And now, it seemed, it was happening all over again.

Maybe I should pray for a girl, Synnamon thought. Conner hadn't said anything about the baby's sex. Maybe that meant it didn't matter—or maybe he was enough like her father that only a son would do. Maybe he hadn't even considered the possibility that his child could be a girl.

If that was so, and the baby was a daughter, he might vanish from their lives, after all. As, for all intents and purposes, Silas Sherwood had turned his back on his daughter.

It had been so simple, Synnamon thought wearily. It had all made such perfect sense. She and Conner didn't want to be married, so the sensible thing—the only civilized thing—was to split. But there would be no recriminations, no anger, no fights. No bitterness, no resentment, no tugs-of-war over money or possessions. Theirs would be the perfect divorce.

But now, because she had stupidly lost control of herself in a moment of pain and loneliness and created a life that would link the two of them forever, their perfect divorce was falling apart.

CHAPTER FIVE

SYNNAMON didn't get out of bed on the morning after New Year's Day before she reached for the telephone and called Morea Landon's law office.

Morea's secretary sounded doubtful. "She's due in court this morning, Mrs. Welles, and she may not even come to the office first. But the moment she arrives I'll tell her you called."

"Tell her," Synnamon said firmly, "that it's urgent."

She felt a little better knowing she'd done everything she could for the moment. And her morning sickness seemed to have taken the day off, she discovered when she cautiously stood up.

She rummaged through her closet for jeans and a sweater. It felt strange to dress so informally on a week-day morning, when her normal attire would be a tailored suit and heels and panty hose. In fact, she was tempted to stick to her terry robe and scuffed slippers, just to make the point to Conner that she wasn't going out of her way to look her best for him. Except, she thought, he probably wouldn't notice.

He was still in the apartment, Synnamon had no doubt of that. She could feel his presence, even though it was past the time he usually arrived at the office.

Mrs. Ogden was back from her holiday, and when Synnamon reached the kitchen the housekeeper was just setting a plate of waffles and sausage on the breakfast bar in front of Conner.

"That looks wonderful, Mrs. O," he said, and the housekeeper beamed.

"Don't let him fool you into waiting on him," Synnamon murmured. "He's perfectly capable of taking care of himself."

Mrs. Ogden clicked her tongue in reproof. "But where's the fun in that, Mrs. Welles? And what would you like for breakfast this morning?"

"Just fruit and coffee. I'll get it myself."

Mrs. Ogden poured Synnamon's coffee, however, and set it on the breakfast bar directly across from Conner's plate. She took the opportunity to top off Conner's cup, as well. "Yes," she said with a broad smile as if picking up a conversation where Synnamon had interrupted it. "It certainly is nice to see you back where you belong, Mr. Welles. Such a nice young couple you two make."

Behind the open refrigerator door, Synnamon rolled her eyes heavenward. She was selecting a grapefruit when the telephone rang, and Mrs. Ogden reached it first. "One moment, please," she said disapprovingly, and held it out to Synnamon. "It's that Ms. Landon, for you."

Conner's eyebrows lifted, but he didn't comment, just cut another bite of waffle.

Synnamon seized the phone. "Morea, I'm on the cordless phone, but let me run to another room, all right?"

"Only if you hurry," Morea said. "I'm sorry, but I've got just two minutes before I have to leave for court. I would have put you off till afternoon if Cindy hadn't said it was urgent, because the unbearable Ridge Coltrain is waiting for me."

Synnamon let the kitchen door swing shut behind her, but she still wasn't far enough from Conner and Mrs. Ogden to feel safe. "Did you put garlic in your scrambled eggs this morning just for him?"

Morea sniffed. "Why bother? I had heartburn for a day and a half after that episode, and he didn't even turn a hair. Then just as our conference was ending he complimented me on my new perfume. Can you imagine? Why do you have to leave the room to talk on your own phone, anyway? Is Mrs. Ogden spying for the opposition? What's wrong, darling?"

Synnamon had reached the relative safety of the big living room. "I'm pregnant, Morea."

Fifteen seconds of dead silence ticked by before Morea said, "That's urgent, all right. I'm afraid I can't speed up the divorce, though, if that's what you're calling about. We're locked into that timetable unless everybody agrees to move things up, and I can't just go to Conner's attorney without giving a reason for the hurry, so—"

Synnamon took a deep breath and interrupted. "It's not that at all, Morea."

"Oh? I assumed you'd want to marry the father as soon as possible."

"Not exactly," Synnamon said dryly.

"Surely you aren't asking *me* to tell Conner? As a matter of fact, there's no reason for him even to know—"

"I've already told him. And there was every reason."

There was another brief silence. "Oh, no," Morea said wearily. "I don't think I want to hear this."

"It...just sort of happened. When we were in Phoenix."

Morea sighed. "Have I ever told you you're the single most difficult client I've ever dealt with, Synnamon Welles? No, I take that back—not because it isn't true, but because that sort of comment is unethical and unprofessional and could get me censured if you complained to the bar association."

"I wouldn't."

"Now that's an isolated example of good judgment. Nobody else would take you on. Dammit, Synnamon, if you'd been scheming to take a simple divorce and mess it up, you couldn't have done a better job!"

"Believe me, this wasn't *my* idea." A vague doubt flickered momentarily through Synnamon's mind, but she promptly dismissed it. She was being silly—far too suspicious for her own good. Conner couldn't have planned this set of circumstances any more than she could have, and if anything he would have had less reason.

Morea had regained her self-control. "All right. I really have to go to court this instant, but I'll meet you for lunch at the Pinnacle and we'll talk it over."

"Not the Pinnacle," Synnamon pleaded. "Somewhere I can keep both feet firmly on the ground. Can we make it Maxie's instead?"

"All right. One o'clock."

"Thanks, Morea."

"And Synnamon—don't do anything idiotic between now and then, all right?"

"Like what?"

"I couldn't possibly recite a full list," Morea said wryly. "So let's just say, don't do *anything*."

The phone clicked in Synnamon's ear. She turned the receiver off.

"How's Morea?" Conner asked pleasantly.

Synnamon jumped a foot. She wheeled toward the foyer to see him leaning against the French door. "How long have you been standing there?"

"Long enough. But don't worry, you didn't say anything incriminating, or even suggestive. Actually, I was just waiting till you got off the phone to tell you goodbye, as any good husband would."

"Oh, cut out the role-playing," Synnamon said crossly.

"Or get some acting lessons, if you want to be credible as a loving spouse."

"I'll keep that in mind." His voice was calm. "So what did your attorney advise?"

"Do you think I'm going to tell you?"

"Of course not. But you might think about it long and hard before you talk to her again, Synnamon. This isn't a rag doll we're talking about, you know—it's a real little human being who deserves the best start in life we can give him."

"Or her," she said sweetly.

Conner didn't comment. "I happen to believe that includes two full-time parents. And I also suspect that if you'll let yourself simmer down long enough to really think about it, you'll admit I'm right." Conner reached into the closet for his trench coat.

"Two full-time antagonistic parents, you mean? At each others' throats all the time, and wretchedly miserable?"

"Of course not. I'm not expecting us to act like lovebirds, any more than we ever did. But look at it this way, Synnamon. If we could agree so easily to a cool and civilized divorce, surely we can agree to resume a cool and civilized marriage."

"It is *not* the same thing," Synnamon argued.

He raised his eyebrows a trifle. "Is there someone in your life that I should know about?"

"I don't have to have another man on the string in order to want a divorce, Conner."

He smiled. "I didn't think there was."

Synnamon didn't know if she was more annoyed at herself for taking the bait or at him for the implication that she couldn't possibly attract another man. And before she could decide, Conner was gone.

She swore under her breath and went to the kitchen for her grapefruit and coffee.

Mrs. Ogden was cleaning the breakfast bar. "It does my heart good to see that man back where he belongs," she said once more. "I suspected you were regretting the decision you'd made, the way you've moped around the place for the last month or so."

"Moped?" Synnamon said coolly.

Mrs. Ogden nodded. "Ever since the Contessa died, I've wondered if you weren't having second thoughts about asking Mr. Welles to leave. That's the kind of thing that certainly makes one think, a loss like that. And then when you told me you were quitting your job, I said to myself this was in the wind, that you'd finally seen how much more important your husband is than that work of yours."

Synnamon stared at her, bemused. She'd always known Mrs. Ogden was a romantic, but she'd never realized how rosily unrealistic the woman could be. Had she honestly been unaware of the tension in the kitchen this morning?

"What shall I make for dinner, do you think?" Mrs. Ogden rinsed out her dishcloth and started to work on the range. "Oh, I know—my beef bourguignonne is Mr. Welles's favorite, and I can leave it to simmer when I go home, so all you'll have to do is dish it up." She gave Synnamon a conspiratorial smile. "And don't worry about cleaning up the mess afterward. Shall I put candles on the dining room table, or would you rather eat by the fireplace?"

Synnamon pushed her coffee away. It had gotten cold, and she'd lost her taste for it, anyway. "Whatever you like. If you'll excuse me, Mrs. Ogden, I have to go change my clothes."

"For what? You look fine to me."

Synnamon paused in the doorway. "Because I'm going to work after all, that's why."

Mrs. Ogden's mouth fell open, and instantly Synnamon regretted her sharpness. Being annoyed with Conner was one thing. Taking it out on the good-hearted Mrs. Ogden was something else.

Then the housekeeper smiled. "I think it's cute," she said, "that you just can't stand the idea of not seeing him till dinnertime."

Morea Landon was already at Maxie's Bar, stirring a glass of tomato juice with a celery stick, when Synnamon dropped into the chair across from her.

"Sorry I'm late," Synnamon said. "An impossible client."

"Now why does that problem sound familiar?" Morea murmured. "I thought you were finished with impossible clients. Don't tell me Conner still hasn't hired anyone to fill your job."

Synnamon waved a hand. "As a matter of fact, he has, but I'll tell you all about that later. Am I the reason you're scowling at that poor glass of tomato juice?"

"Aren't you enough cause? I come back from a wonderful week on the ski slopes to find my only straightforward case has suddenly taken on as many twists as a plate of noodles. To tell you the truth, I'm wishing the tomato juice was Ridge Coltrain's blood, but we can save that story for later, too. Tell me what on earth made you lose your mind."

Synnamon sighed. "I was upset about the Contessa, of course. It was the night before she died, and Conner was right there, and I just wanted to—"

"I didn't mean I wanted the details about *that* bit of insanity," Morea said hastily. "I have an imagination, after all. But why didn't you tell me before you went blabbing the news to Conner?''

Synnamon shrugged. ''It just seemed the fair thing to do.''

''I'm your attorney, Synnamon. How can I advise you if—''

''And he's the baby's father, Morea. Doesn't that give him some rights?''

Morea looked a bit abashed.

More gently, Synnamon went on, ''Besides, you were in Telluride—and I thought Conner would be reasonable.''

''But he wasn't, of course. What did he say?''

''It wasn't what he said,'' Synnamon said carefully, ''so much as what he did. He moved in.''

Morea dropped her celery stick into her glass, and tomato juice splashed across her cream-colored sweater. She didn't seem to notice. ''Into the apartment, you mean? And you let him? Synnamon—''

''A lot I had to say about it,'' Synnamon said acidly. ''I just blinked and there he was. Now I want to know how—''

Morea shook her head and stared over Synnamon's shoulder, her wide, dark eyes intent.

There was no missing the message. Synnamon bit off the rest of her sentence and turned to look over her shoulder.

The maître d' was seating a solitary guest at the next table. Synnamon sighed. ''Fancy meeting you here, Conner.''

''Hello, Synnamon—and Morea, too.''

He was trying, she thought, to look just a trifle worried. Synnamon wasn't convinced for a moment. There was no doubt in her mind he'd overheard her this morning arranging to meet Morea at Maxie's. The only question she had was how he'd been so certain of the time.

"I hope my presence doesn't blight your conversation," he said. "I *could* ask for a different table, I suppose, but as busy as the restaurant is today..."

"Oh, come on over and join us," Morea said. "Let's take care of this right now."

Conner moved without apparent haste, but so smoothly that before Synnamon could gather the words to protest he'd taken the chair next to hers and was signaling the waiter to bring him a glass of water. "You don't know how happy this makes me, Morea," he said earnestly.

Synnamon's inner alarm system was shrieking warnings. What did he have to be happy about?

Morea said dryly, "I'm sure you're going to tell me why, Conner."

"I know, you see, that last week the three of us couldn't have had any sort of formal conference. We'd have needed my attorney present to protect my rights."

"True enough," Morea said. "And furthermore, we *still*—"

"So, since you invited me over to chat, that must mean that you're no longer Synnamon's attorney." He smiled. "And since I fired my lawyer this morning, too—" He reached for Synnamon's hand.

She moved it just in time. He was a better actor, she thought, than she'd given him credit for being.

"The least I can do to celebrate," he went on, "is to buy you both lunch. Oh, and send your bill to me, Morea—I'll settle it up immediately, and then we can simply be friends again."

Morea stared at him for a few seconds, then turned to Synnamon. "I apologize," she murmured. "Now I see what you meant about *letting* him move in. Stopping him is like arguing with an influenza germ.''

"I'm glad you realize it," Conner said. He turned to Synnamon. His eyes were dark and intense. "So the divorce *is* off, then?''

Synnamon closed her menu with a snap. "You can't force me to stay married to you, Conner.''

"I can certainly make it costly for you to divorce me.''

Morea frowned. "No more than it already has been, I'd say.''

"Perhaps not, if all you're talking about is money. But since that's not the only question now...''

Synnamon's heart twisted. "You told me you wouldn't ask for custody. Fool that I was, I believed you!''

"I said it wouldn't be my first choice," he corrected. "But if you force me, Synnamon, I will do whatever is necessary. I will not be reduced to a footnote in my child's life.'' He shook his napkin out with a snap and draped it across the edge of the table. "It's your choice, Synnamon. Let me know what you decide. I don't think, however, that I'll stay for lunch after all.''

He left behind a silence thicker than Maxie's famous cream of mushroom soup.

Finally, Synnamon asked, "He *can't* get custody, can he?''

For a moment, she thought Morea wasn't going to answer. Then the attorney sighed. "It's hard to tell. The fascination of the law, of course, is that there are two sides to every question, and you never know what a judge will decide in a particular case. Even when there's clear precedent for a mother's request—''

"Thanks for the encouragement," Synnamon said wryly.

"Sorry, darling, but I'm just doing my job. If I guaranteed results, I'd be crazy." Morea added thoughtfully, "And probably disbarred, too."

"If you'd tell a judge the things Conner said just now, the threats he made…"

"What threats? All I heard him say is that he intends to be involved in his child's life, and I can't think of a single divorce-court judge who wouldn't burst into applause at that announcement. Besides, I can't exactly testify to anything, because I'm not only your attorney but a prejudiced witness. It would be pretty easy for the court to dismiss my opinion."

"Then what do I do? Just go on with it and take my chances?"

Morea's eyes narrowed. "There is one possibility."

"I'm willing to try anything."

"It might not solve the problem entirely, of course. But if Conner were to change his mind—"

Synnamon started to laugh. "Oh, please. That's what you call a possibility? If Conner set out to empty the Pacific Ocean with a soup ladle, I wouldn't bet against him. Morea, if that's the best you can do—"

Morea shrugged. "It's the only thing I can think of. The whole idea of divorce makes people do strange things. I've known couples who hated each other, but they simply couldn't keep their distance because the joy each of them got from annoying their partner was more satisfying than having a scrap of peace for themselves."

"I don't see Conner being that sort."

"No, but the principle still applies. You want him to move out of your apartment but also to give up the idea of custody, right? Well, arguing about either matter is only going to make him more determined about both. I've seen it happen in a hundred cases, with men a lot less stubborn than Conner is. But if *he's* the one who gives up the idea of staying married, if he's forced to admit that this grand idea of his simply won't work..."

The silence drew out into forever while Synnamon thought about it. "And just what do you think I can do to make that happen?"

"At the moment," Morea admitted, "I haven't a clue."

Annie looked pathetically glad to see Synnamon. "I'm glad you're back," she said. "This afternoon there have already been half a dozen people who wanted to talk to you. And one of them—"

Synnamon hung her suit jacket in the closet. "That's easily explained." Her voice was matter-of-fact. "Once they find out I'm gone, they'll be quite happy to have your attention instead."

"You mean one head of customer relations is just the same as another?" Annie asked skeptically.

"Well, perhaps not quite. But all you need is the benefit of the doubt for a few weeks till you have a chance to prove yourself, and they'll be eager to talk to you."

"I wish I believed you were right. But one of them hung up on me just now when I explained you weren't with the company any more—and I think he was going to call Mr. Welles directly."

"Who was it?"

Annie reached for a pink message slip, but she didn't look at it. The name was obviously engraved on her brain. "Luigi." She sounded like the voice of doom.

"The one who owns the string of beauty spas?"

"There can't be more than one with a single name and an Italian accent thick enough to slice, can there?"

"I hope not. Luigi's an original—a truly self-made man. His real name is Harold Henderson, and my father told me once that he was born in the south Bronx. I wouldn't worry about him, Annie. I'm sure Mr. Welles will be up to the challenge of dealing with Luigi.''

"You don't *mind* if he talks to Mr. Welles? It's not you he'll be complaining about, of course, it's me, but—''

"I wouldn't be so certain of that. Luigi has a tendency to take everything personally, so he's probably feeling insulted by the fact I'm leaving.''

"Oh, now that's a real comfort,'' Annie said wryly.

"Relax. It's just part of his stereotypical vision of how a temperamental Italian should behave.''

"Well, it doesn't change the fact that his account is the size of the national debt, and if he calls Mr. Welles and makes a fuss about how I treated him…''

"It's not you, Annie. He just hates change. He complained about me when I first took the job, too.''

"I suppose that should make me feel better,'' Annie admitted. "But since that was before Mr. Welles's time… Does he know about Harold Henderson and the south Bronx?''

"I'm sure he does, but I'll remind him.''

"Would you? *Can* you? I mean…''

"No doubt,'' Synnamon said dryly, "Conner and I will exchange words from time to time.''

Annie sighed. "Then you're still… Even with the baby… Sorry. I didn't mean to be nosy.''

Synnamon started to announce that of course there would be no change in plans. Instead, she heard herself saying softly, "I'm not sure what's going to happen.''

The sudden uncertainty startled her, but she had to admit it was the only honest reaction she was capable of just now. She was too confused to know what to do.

She knew, intellectually, that Morea was right. The only way Synnamon could achieve her long-term goals was for Conner to change his mind. Arguing obviously wouldn't accomplish that. It was likely to make Conner more stubborn. But reasoning with him wasn't going to work, either. She'd already tried that approach. And if she simply went along with what he suggested, and resumed their farce of a marriage... Well, Conner had seemed perfectly comfortable in that role before, so what was to prevent him from settling down into it once more?

Synnamon was the only variable—or at least the only one she could control. She'd have to make sure he wasn't so complacent this time around.

An idea stirred to life at the back of her mind and slowly took shape. What would happen if *she* became the complacent one—or, at least, if she appeared to be? If she seemed contented with the situation, placidly accepting how things had worked out, might Conner begin to feel restless? Uneasy? Even, perhaps, eager to be free?

"Hand me the phone," she told Annie.

"Are you going to call Mr. Welles about Luigi?"

Synnamon had forgotten all about Luigi. "Why not?" she murmured. "He'll make a lovely excuse. But first..."

Conner was waiting for her. The door of his office was open, and he was perched on the corner of his secretary's desk, signing letters, when Synnamon came into the waiting room.

To a casual observer, she thought, he would appear perfectly at ease. Even Carol probably couldn't tell the difference. But Synnamon could feel the tension in the lean lines of his body. And of course the fact that he was in the outer office at all was a dead giveaway.

He's eager to talk to me, she thought, and her pulse went into overdrive.

She hadn't told Carol what her business was, just that she needed a little time with Conner. She'd been counting on having a couple of quiet minutes to gather her thoughts before confronting him. Now, robbed of that island of serenity, she felt her mouth going dry with anticipation.

He signed the last letter, handed the clipboard to the secretary and stood up. "Hold my calls, please, Carol. Synnamon…" His gesture toward the open office door was a wordless invitation.

She accepted it silently and told herself it was foolish to be anxious. Either this idea would work—eventually— or it wouldn't. If it didn't, she would be no worse off than she was at the moment.

Still, she couldn't quite stop her insides from quivering.

Conner waved a hand toward the couch. "Make yourself comfortable. What can I do for you?"

Synnamon settled into the corner of the love seat. Her pastel tweed skirt slid slowly upward. Her fingers twitched with the urge to pull it down, but she forced her hands to stay still, folded in her lap, instead. To give her skirt a nervous tug would carry a twofold message. It would say first that she was jittery around him—which was true enough but was hardly a thought she wanted to cross Conner's mind. Second, it would imply that she expected him to be watching, and perhaps even wanted him to be interested in the view of her knees—which was far from the truth, and again not something she wanted Conner to be thinking about.

"What can I do for you?" he asked.

She raised her gaze to his face. "Have you talked to Luigi lately?"

She wasn't disappointed. Surprise flickered in his face, and his eyes shadowed from blue to intensely purple. She had to admire his control, however. An instant later there was no evidence he'd been so much as startled. "Not for a couple of weeks. Why?"

She told him about Annie's encounter with the spa owner. "He threatened to call you, and naturally she's concerned that you might blame her for upsetting him. I told her you understood Luigi's point of view—"

"Without a doubt."

"And his history, and that you wouldn't have any trouble handling his complaints."

"Your confidence in me is touching, Synnamon. I'll certainly give it my best effort. Thanks for the warning."

"My pleasure."

"Is there anything else?"

"No, I don't think so." She stood up. "Oh, yes—there is. Something I've always wondered." She paused, letting curiosity have a chance to grow. "Is there really a bed built into this office?"

To her disappointment, Conner's eyebrows didn't even twitch. "If so, it's too well hidden for me to find. Or are you suggesting that I install one?"

"Certainly not for my sake," Synnamon said politely. "I was just wondering. You won't be late tonight, will you?"

She thought she saw wariness creep into his eyes, but all he said was, "I was planning to stop by the hotel first, pick up my clothes and check out."

He hadn't already done that? So he hadn't been nearly as sure of himself as he'd been acting, Synnamon thought, and annoyance chewed at the corners of her mind. Perhaps, if she'd held firm just a little longer instead of acting on Morea's advice...

"But I'm sure that will take only a few minutes," Conner went on smoothly.

It was too late to back out, Synnamon knew. She was embarked on this new path, and she'd have to see it through. "It's beef bourguignonne," she said. "Mrs. Ogden and I decided since it was your favorite…"

"Then I'll try to hurry—" he paused "—home."

"Good." Synnamon allowed herself a smile. That tiny hesitation of his had spoken volumes. Her self-confidence took a gigantic leap. All she had to do was be sweet, innocent and accommodating—up to a point—and before long Conner would be choking on his grand idea.

"Because I've invited a guest," she went on. "She'll be there at seven o'clock."

"She?" There was a note of distrust in Conner's voice.

Synnamon had to make an effort to hide her delight at the reaction. "Yes," she said gently. "Since she's going to be working here at Sherwood, I thought perhaps I should get to know her better. I hope you don't mind spending an entire evening with Nicole Fox?"

CHAPTER SIX

THE apartment was dim and quiet when Synnamon let herself in. The thin gray daylight was gone, as was Mrs. Ogden. But true to her promise, the housekeeper had left the bourguignonne simmering in the oven, and its scent wafted down the hall to greet Synnamon.

She was happy to see that Mrs. Ogden had opted for the dining room instead of setting up an intimate meal before the fireplace. The table was covered with starched white linen and half a dozen candles. Two silver service plates had been polished to a gleam and laid at a corner of the table, ready for the dinner plates to be put in place.

It was very thoughtful of Mrs. Ogden to arrange it that way, Synnamon decided, so it would be possible for the two diners to stare into each others' eyes without blinding themselves with the candlelight. And the housekeeper had added white ribbons, and something that looked like orange blossom.

Synnamon shook her head with wry humor as she got another service plate from the cabinet and set it at the opposite end of the table from the other two. The idea of inviting Nicole Fox was looking better and better. Set for three, the dining room had a pleasant party atmosphere. As a twosome, it would look positively bridal—which of course was exactly what Mrs. Ogden had in mind.

Synnamon frowned. One thing she and Conner hadn't talked about was whether he intended to move into the master bedroom as well as the apartment.

Surely he wouldn't even suggest it, she thought. He'd

hardly spent any time there when the marriage was still a real one, and now that it was purely a nominal relationship...

She frowned again as she went to the kitchen to stir the bourguignonne. She was just sliding the dish into the oven when the doorbell rang. It was seven o'clock on the dot, and standing on the welcome mat was Nicole Fox.

She looked just a bit pale, Synnamon thought, and very wary. Of course, that was no surprise. She'd been practically speechless this afternoon when Synnamon had phoned her to issue the invitation.

Nicole stepped into the foyer and gave up her coat with what Synnamon couldn't help but interpret as reluctance. Her gaze darted across the hall into the obviously empty living room, and Synnamon had no trouble following the path of her thoughts. As a matter of fact, she was thinking the same thing herself. *Where was Conner?*

Surely, she thought, he wouldn't leave her to entertain Nicole Fox alone. It wasn't that he'd feel obligated to appear, exactly. She could even imagine him saying that since she hadn't consulted him before inviting a guest, she could hardly rely on him to help her entertain.

But she didn't think it likely he would risk it, under the circumstances. He couldn't know what she might have planned for the evening, and surely he wouldn't dare leave the two of them without a buffer.

However, Synnamon supposed she might have miscalculated. Perhaps he had enough faith in Nicole to leave her on her own with the problematic wife. They might have been together somewhere just now, snatching a few moments of privacy and making plans for how to handle Synnamon. She could almost hear the conversation.

"What's she up to, anyway?"

"I don't know, we'll have to just play along."

"Maybe she suspects?"

Oh, stop it, Synnamon told herself. She was starting to sound like a bad spy movie!

"Conner isn't home yet," she said lightly as she led Nicole into the big living room, where the gas fire was already giving off a pleasant wave of warmth. "He had some things to do after he left the office, I think. Would you like a Scotch and water?"

The redhead nodded. "What a beautiful view you have of the mountains."

Mrs. Ogden had left a tray on the cocktail table, Synnamon noticed, something she hadn't done since Conner had moved out. Before that, it had been a daily routine, even though much of the time the tray had gone untouched. After Conner had left, Synnamon had told the housekeeper to stop. It was one more reminder she didn't need.

The scary part, however, wasn't that Mrs. Ogden had so easily returned to the routine of the old days, but that Synnamon had turned automatically to look for the tray. Perhaps it would be easier than she thought to slide into the old ways. Not that she wanted to, of course. But maybe Conner wasn't so far off track about thinking this cool and civilized marriage could work.

Nicole held the cocktail glass Synnamon handed her, but she didn't take a sip.

Synnamon poured herself a champagne flute full of club soda and dropped in a wedge of lime. She settled into a wing chair by the window and gestured to the matching one opposite her. "Please sit down. It *is* a wonderful view, isn't it? I think that's what made me choose this apartment over every other one I looked at before Conner and I were married."

Nicole nodded and obediently sat, but she didn't answer.

For nearly twenty minutes Synnamon kept the conversation going, moving from one innocuous subject to the next—but it was some of the hardest work she had ever done. Nicole seemed to consider every response at great length.

Synnamon heard Conner's key the instant it clicked into the lock, and a wave of relief swept over her. She was puzzled for an instant by her reaction. She certainly wasn't particularly happy to see him. His presence wasn't going to make the situation delightful or her own role any less guarded. In fact, the tension level could only increase with him there. And that was why she'd planned the evening in the first place, wasn't it?

But at least she wouldn't be stuck trying to pry a few words out of a silent dinner companion. And at least she'd be able to add a little discomfort to his life as well as her own, and if she was lucky, that uneasiness would make him start to question his decision.

"Hello, dear," he said calmly as he came across the living room. "Good to see you, Nick." He bent over Synnamon's chair before she had considered what he might do. Almost reflexively she jerked her head, and his lips brushed across her hair. Synnamon was annoyed with herself. He'd intended to kiss her temple, she was sure. It wasn't as if he'd planned some passionate display. She ought to have stayed perfectly still, not tried to dodge him like a nervous virgin.

He shook Nicole's hand, and smiled.

Synnamon was greatly impressed with his self-control, less so with the way Nicole's eyes widened and fastened on him as if she was a drowning sailor who'd just glimpsed a life belt.

"Shall I fix you a drink, darling?" Synnamon asked solicitously.

"No, thanks."

She tried to sound casual, perfectly normal, as she launched the next element of her plan. "Then if you'll excuse me, Conner, I'll leave you to entertain our guest until dinner. The bourguignonne needs just a bit of last-minute attention."

Leave them alone, she'd decided, *and see what happens*. Of course, she wasn't naive enough to think that they couldn't arrange to meet anytime they liked. There were opportunities aplenty for that. But the idea of being alone together with the troublesome wife just down the hall had a piquancy that Synnamon thought they could not ignore.

"Is the bourguignonne what I'm smelling?" Nicole asked just as Synnamon left the room. Conner must have nodded, for she went on, "It's a wonderful aroma. Just think of the potential if we could reproduce that for a kitchen air freshener, Conner."

She was laughing a little, but there was a catch in Nicole's voice when she said his name that sent a quiver up Synnamon's spine.

Synnamon told herself it was nothing out of line, exactly. It was so subtle that if she hadn't been listening for something of the sort, she probably would have passed it over. It wasn't as if Nicole was in obvious pain...

She began to feel a little ashamed of herself for dragging Nicole into this. It might not have been smart of the woman to get involved at any level with a man who was still technically married—but it wasn't exactly her fault, either. Who could have predicted this twist of events?

Synnamon served the broiled grapefruit appetizer, and when she went into the living room Conner and Nicole were talking about the research and development team. There was something a bit strained about the conversation, Synnamon thought, but at least Nicole was talking.

Conner held a chair for Nicole and then came around the table to help Synnamon, but she'd pretended not to notice and had already seated herself. "How has the response been from the other chemists?" she asked as she spread her napkin carefully across her lap and picked up her grapefruit spoon.

"There's been some grumbling," Conner said. "Not as much as you expected there would be, however—mostly because, with your warning in mind, I made it clear from the start that I wouldn't tolerate it."

The note of approval—almost appreciation—in his voice startled Synnamon.

"I think even that will die down once Nick really gets started." He smiled at the redhead. "Once they see what she can do…"

Was there something a little more than friendly about that smile? Synnamon asked, "When will you start to work, Nicole?"

"I have to give a month's notice to my current employer."

Synnamon frowned.

"Is something wrong?" Conner asked.

"I was just thinking that it might have been wiser to wait to make the announcement," Synnamon mused. "Giving them a month to think about it, without the new boss present…"

"Oh, Nick will be in and out. And I have no doubt she can handle anything that bunch might do or say."

Nicole looked less certain, Synnamon thought. That was odd. At the New Year's Eve party she'd seemed to ooze confidence. But of course, things had changed since New Year's—and not only where the job was concerned.

"The situation will have difficulties," Nicole said. "But I'm looking forward to the challenge."

"I'm sure you'll do very well," Synnamon said. It was almost a throwaway line, a social nicety, but it was true, she realized. It had always been the other members of the team she was concerned about, not Nicole herself. For no matter what Conner thought of her personally, he wouldn't have given her the job if she wasn't an able chemist.

Synnamon was startled when Nicole looked up from her grapefruit with a sudden smile that lit her eyes and turned her good looks into stunning beauty.

"You wouldn't like to put that in the company newsletter, I suppose?" Nicole said.

Still a bit bemused by the woman's sparkle, Synnamon said slowly, "I don't quite know what you mean."

"You see, it's obvious that your opinion is very important to everyone at Sherwood."

Involuntarily, Synnamon's gaze slid down the length of the table to find Conner watching her thoughtfully over the rim of his wineglass.

Almost everyone, she nearly said. *Except perhaps the boss*. Instead, she shrugged. "Since I'm not officially on the payroll any more, I can't see it making much of a difference. But if I can help—"

"Of course you can," Conner said. "A few simple things should do it. You could have lunch together a few times, maybe."

Synnamon would have given anything to be able to glare at him and announce that she had no intention of becoming friends with Nicole Fox. But to say so would be to admit that she wasn't any more comfortable with the situation he'd created than Conner was.

In fact, she thought irritably, at the moment she was probably less at ease. How did the man do it, anyway? It wasn't fair that he could turn the tables on her so completely and so effortlessly.

Somehow talking about the new job had broken the ice, and Nicole seemed to relax. Suspiciously, Synnamon replayed the conversation as she served the bourguignonne. She couldn't help wondering if the whole thing had really been coincidence or if she'd been conned—manipulated into a public position of friendship.

Despite her best efforts to stay aloof, however, she found herself liking Nicole Fox. Though she was still quiet, the woman displayed a dry sense of humor, and under the influence of the bourguignonne she laughed now and then.

Eventually, Synnamon put her napkin down and began to clear the table. ''I'll be happy to help,'' Nicole offered.

''Oh, no.'' Synnamon smiled. ''You've been very restrained, both of you, in not discussing chemistry over dinner, and I appreciate it. So I'll leave you to it for a few minutes while the coffee brews.''

She loaded the dishwasher and sliced the chocolate cheesecake, and as soon as the coffee was finished, she loaded a tray and carried it into the living room.

She honestly wasn't trying to be silent, but she succeeded better than she could have hoped. Conner and Nicole had moved to the wide bay window, where only a darker line marked the Rockies in the distance and a golden web of lights spread out across the high plain below the apartment tower. The redhead's hand was on Conner's sleeve, and she was looking at him intently. Her voice was low, but Synnamon had no trouble catching the words. "Are you quite sure you want to go through with this, Conner? You're obviously miserable, and it isn't likely to get easier."

Conner didn't answer. Something caught his attention—Synnamon's reflection in the window glass, perhaps—and he shook Nicole's hand off his sleeve and came hastily across the room to take the tray from Synnamon's hands. "You shouldn't be carrying things like this," he said.

"Why not? It weighs less than my briefcase does."

"Then you shouldn't be carrying that, either."

The irritation in his voice pleased Synnamon beyond all reason. Nicole's question had obviously ruffled his composure, and that alone made the strain of the evening worthwhile.

Nicole looked uncomfortable. "I'm surprised you don't have someone to help around the house," she said finally.

So we're all just going to ignore that leading question, Synnamon thought with satisfaction, *and pretend it was never asked*. Well, that was all right with her—a question with no answer was an even more haunting one. It wouldn't bother her any if it kept Conner awake all night.

"Only during the day," she said. "Mrs. Ogden has never lived in. We treasure our privacy—I'm sure you understand. Do you take cream and sugar in your coffee, Nicole?"

Synnamon was sorry to see the evening end. She had to admit, however, that it wasn't entirely because of that spark of liking that had sprung to life between her and Nicole Fox, but because she wasn't looking forward to facing the music once she and Conner were alone.

She left him to finish the good nights, even suggesting that he walk Nicole down to her car, and retreated to the kitchen to attack the mess. She'd put the silver flatware to soak and was in the dining room, stacking the last of the china on a tray, when Conner returned.

It hadn't been as long a farewell as she'd expected, and she had to bite her tongue to keep from asking what had brought him back so quickly. But it was best for her plan to appear not to notice at all.

He brushed her aside and picked up the tray. "You aren't to be lifting things like this any more."

The order annoyed her. "Says who? I'm not handicapped, I'm having a baby. And if you think me lifting a few pieces of china is going to hurt *your child*..."

"Would you rather I call Phoenix and ask the Hartfords to move up here and take over?"

"Of course not."

"Then you'll behave yourself."

Synnamon went on as if he hadn't said anything. "There's no room for them."

"There's a housekeeper's suite."

"*Suite*? A bedroom and a tiny bath are hardly the sort of accommodation they're used to." She followed him to the kitchen and cleared a spot on the counter for the tray. "If what you're really saying is that you'd be more comfortable with someone else around all the time so we're never alone—"

His eyebrows drew together. "Is that why you invited Nick to dinner? Because you don't want to be alone with me?"

Synnamon bit the tip of her tongue. It was just like him to take a straightforward comment and turn it around. "I didn't say anything of the sort. I just thought it would be nice to get to know her better. I had no idea you'd object. But as long as we're getting things straight, perhaps you'll let me know what rules you'd like to set up."

"Does that mean you have some in mind?"

"Well, yes. They're not much different from the ones you'd propose, I'm sure. For instance, don't feel that you have to account for yourself to me, any more than you do to your secretary."

"Oh, I'll happily keep you informed of all my plans," Conner murmured.

What if I'd rather not know what you're up to? Synnamon almost said it, but she bit the words off in time. That was hardly the way to convince him there would be no satisfaction in sacrificing his freedom just to annoy her.

"If you like," she said mildly. "I'll be happy to listen, of course." She started to wash the silver flatware. "I thought you were going to get your clothes and things tonight."

"I did. I left them downstairs with the doorman, because I didn't think you'd be pleased if I staggered in carrying a load of suitcases while Nick was here. Which reminds me, I'll have to call and have him bring them up."

He picked up the house phone.

The soapy silver was sensually slick in Synnamon's hands, and the rhythmic motion of cleaning each piece combined with the rise and fall of Conner's voice in a pleasant pattern.

Overall, she decided, she was happy with the evening. It hadn't turned out quite as she'd hoped, that was true, mostly because of Conner's uncomfortable tendency to twist anything she said around to his own interpretation. But even the fact that he was suspicious and prone to attack surely illustrated the effectiveness of her campaign. He was off-balance and ill at ease. Obviously he didn't know quite what to think.

Perhaps, Synnamon thought dreamily, *if I can keep on giving him the sweetly reasonable, noninterfering, slightly dull wife he seems to want, he might soon decide he doesn't want her after all.*

She finished the flatware and reached for the first crystal wine goblet, laying it carefully in the soapy water.

Or maybe she should go one step further. If she could convincingly portray a clinging vine who was threatening to smother him in unwanted attention, Conner would probably run for cover.

No, she decided, she could never carry that one off.

Conner put the house phone down. "Jack's on his way up. Where shall I have him put my things, Synnamon? In the guest suite—or in our bedroom?"

The wineglass Synnamon had just picked up slipped out of her soapy hands and shattered against the edge of the sink. Crystal fragments sliced through the bubbles and rattled against the stainless steel. Almost automatically Synnamon scooped both hands into the water to retrieve the pieces.

Instantly, Conner was beside her, pulling her away from the sink. "Stop it, Synnamon! The goblet is gone, and you'll cut yourself to ribbons for nothing."

"That was Waterford crystal. And it was a wedding gift."

"Well, now it's only broken glass. Watch out for your hands." He gathered her hands into his, cupping them between his palms to inspect each line, each joint for cuts.

His fingers felt cool against her skin after the intense heat of the dishwater. The contrast was like a sudden wave of cold running straight up Synnamon's arms to paralyze her brain.

"I'm dripping suds all over the floor," she said, only half-conscious of what she was saying.

"The floor will survive." Conner raised her hands almost to his face, turning the palms as if to cup them against his jaw. Synnamon thought a bit breathlessly that it was almost as though he intended to kiss her fingertips, soap and all.

"Your hands are like silk," he said, and stroked the edge of her palm with a gentle fingertip.

Synnamon had never realized that the band of skin between her wristbone and the base of her little finger was so sensitive. His touch was as soft as a whisper, but the rhythmic movement sent sensation up her arm in a pattern as distinct and unavoidable as ripples of water across the surface of a pond. Except this rhythm, instead of fading slowly away, intensified with each wave.

"So soft," Conner whispered.

The door bell chimed. To Synnamon's ears, the notes sounded flat and almost harsh, as if the bell had developed a chest cold. Or was it her hearing that had gone berserk?

Idiot, she told herself. He was only holding her hands because of her accident. It was crazy to let herself get carried away. She drew back.

For a moment Conner didn't move. Then he cleared his throat and said pragmatically, "Of course, your hands won't be soft for long if you keep doing dishes without rubber gloves."

"I like to feel what I'm doing."

"But that's Mrs. Ogden's job, isn't it?" He turned toward the foyer and paused. "Guest suite or master bedroom?" She couldn't get a good look at his eyes, and there was not a hint of emotion in his voice—nothing to give her a clue to which answer he would prefer.

Synnamon's fingertips were twitching. With the urge to hit him, she told herself. He'd set her up with absolute perfection. If she asked him to use the guest room, he'd no doubt make some comment about it being a silly choice not to want to share a *room*, since she'd caused the whole problem in the first place by sharing a *bed*. And if she was crazy enough to suggest that he return to the master bedroom—well, wouldn't he have a field day with that invitation!

She had to take a very deep breath before she could say, steadily, "Guest suite."

He didn't answer for a long moment. "Very well. Whatever you prefer."

That's all? Synnamon thought in astonishment. *No smart remarks*? She stared down the hall after him.

She felt almost chilly. The temperature in the kitchen had seemed to drop with his departure, and cool air teased her flushed skin. The twitch in her fingertips hadn't gone away, but she no longer had the urge to strike him. Instead, she could almost feel the smooth strength of his jaw, the faint stubble of his beard, the warmth of his cheek against her palm.

She shook her head in disbelief and turned to the sink, carefully fishing out the broken bits of crystal to discard.

I can't want to touch him, she told herself. *It's insane even to think about holding him, caressing him…making love with him.*

She left a note for Mrs. Ogden to warn her about the bits of broken glass that might remain, dried her hands and started down the long hall to her bedroom.

The door to the guest suite was open. On the bed a suitcase lay open, and Conner was stacking shirts in the armoire. Obviously he heard her, for he paused and turned toward the door as Synnamon approached.

She couldn't just ignore him, of course. That didn't fit at all with the image she was trying to maintain. An image, she reminded herself, that she had come close to ruining a few minutes ago. Standing in the middle of the kitchen going all soft in the head because he was holding her *hands*, for heaven's sake.

She paused in the doorway and said, "I hope you'll be comfortable here, Conner. Good night."

"Synnamon."

"What is it?"

"About this bedroom business," he said gently. "Just let me know when you change your mind."

Mrs. Ogden was so tight-lipped she hardly said good morning at all, and she mopped out the kitchen sink with irritable efficiency.

Synnamon drank her first cup of coffee in silence, studiously ignoring the housekeeper's glare. She was still thinking about Conner's parting shot last night. The sheer gall of the man, to suggest that she would inevitably invite him back into her bed. Hell would freeze before that happened—she'd make good and sure of it.

It didn't help, however, to know that a good deal of her annoyance rose not from Conner's confidence but from her own reactions last night. She wouldn't be nearly as furious if she hadn't caught herself woolgathering about the way his face would feel, slightly rough and bristly against her heat-sensitized hands....

And she was doing it again right now, she reminded herself in exasperation. What on earth was wrong with her?

Mrs. Ogden cleared her throat. "It's not my place to ask, of course," she began.

Synnamon sighed. "Probably not," she agreed. "But what's the problem?"

"I was just wondering if you had a nice evening."

"Just lovely," Synnamon murmured. Her mind slid once more to Conner. *If you keep this up*, she told herself, *there's no longer going to be any doubt about who won the first round. And it's not you, my girl.*

"And did your guest enjoy the bourguignonne?"

Synnamon snapped back to the present. "Guest?"

"There's an extra napkin—covered with lipstick, I might add. *And* you didn't put the silver back quite the way I always do."

So that was what was bothering Mrs. Ogden this morning, Synnamon realized, not the bit of additional laundry, but the fact that the romantic little twosome she'd envisioned hadn't turned out quite as she thought it should. Well, Synnamon thought philosophically, the sooner the housekeeper realized her employers were not exactly Cinderella and her prince, living happily ever after together, the less aggravation she'd cause herself by trying to treat an ordinary apartment as if it was an enchanted castle!

"Yes, she did enjoy it," Synnamon said mildly. "There was plenty, and the flavor was outstanding. It would have been such a shame to waste the extra serving."

Mrs. Ogden grumbled. Synnamon was glad the sudden shrill ring of the telephone kept her from hearing clearly. She ignored the housekeeper and picked up the cordless phone.

"Good morning," Conner said. "Sorry I couldn't stay for breakfast with you."

I'll try to survive the disappointment, Synnamon wanted to say. But sarcasm was guaranteed to get her nowhere. "I hope Mrs. Ogden took good care of you."

"It wasn't the same, of course. I waited as long as I could, but you were sound asleep when I looked in."

He'd looked in on her? *Make a note to put a lock on the bedroom door*, Synnamon ordered herself.

Conner went on, "I was just talking to Hartford, and—"

She exploded. "Dammit, Conner, I told you I don't want them! If you bring them up here, I—I'll fire them!"

"Then it's just as well the subject didn't come up."

She was startled and almost ashamed of herself. "Then why did you call him?"

"I didn't. He phoned me. Actually, he asked for you, but since Annie's new secretary didn't know what to do with him, she transferred the call to my office." His voice dropped into a starkly sober tone. "He asked me to tell you that the Contessa's ashes have been delivered."

Synnamon bit her lip, and tears stung her eyes.

There were times now, six weeks after the Contessa's death, that she could forget the sadness for a few minutes and revel in the happy memories. Sometimes she forgot for a little while that the Contessa was gone. She could pretend that the woman was still only a phone call away, enjoying a balmy winter in Phoenix.

Always, however, something happened to remind her that she could never confide in the Contessa again. This particular reminder was the most painful of blows. The only good thing she could think of was that she could escape from Denver—from Conner—for a few days, and have a chance to think. In Phoenix, surrounded by the Contessa's things and the Contessa's spirit, perhaps she could get hold of herself once more.

"Synnamon? Are you all right?"

She cleared her throat. "Just jolly. What did you expect?"

"I'm sorry."

His voice was husky, and Synnamon regretted her sharp tone. "I'll be all right. I'll need to go to Phoenix, though. She wanted me to take her ashes out to the desert, to a special place she always loved."

"Of course," Conner said. "I'll have Carol get the tickets right away. When shall we go?"

CHAPTER SEVEN

CONNER must have taken her startled silence for assent, for the next thing Synnamon heard was the rustle of pages in his desktop appointment calendar. "It looks to me as if this weekend will work," he said. "I'll have to check with Carol, though, to be sure she hasn't scheduled anything."

Synnamon shook her head, trying to clear her mind. "Conner," she began carefully. "I certainly didn't expect—"

"That I'd let you go alone on such a sad errand," he finished. "Besides, I'd like to pay my final respects, too. I wouldn't feel right, somehow, if I didn't. If I wasn't there, it would seem as if I'd violated the code of ethics that was so important to the Contessa."

Synnamon was left speechless. How could she possibly counter that argument? Of course, the Contessa could probably have punctured his reasoning with her typical good humor. The very thought made Synnamon's eyes sting with tears.

"I'll ask Carol to call you later with the flight details," Conner finished briskly. "And I'll see you this evening. Unless you're planning to come into the office today?"

"I wasn't, but—"

"It's probably as well. Giving Annie a hand is one thing, but she shouldn't start relying on you being here to rescue her every day."

"I'm not rescuing her," Synnamon said crisply. "I'm only lending a hand till she finds her way. And if what you're really saying is that you've already decided she isn't up to the job—''

"Not at all. She seems to be doing fine, with your guidance."

Synnamon didn't answer. While that actually sounded like a compliment, she couldn't quite keep from looking for hidden meanings.

"Sorry," Conner went on. "It was a poor choice of words."

Synnamon sighed. She wondered if her moodiness was because of the pressures of the situation or the raging hormones of early pregnancy. Did she really want to know? One would be over in a few months. The other— if Conner had his way—would go on forever.

"I was a little too sensitive," she said. "I'm sorry, too."

There was a brief silence on the other end of the phone line before Conner said, "Would you like to go out for dinner tonight?"

The invitation startled her, and before she stopped to think Synnamon had answered. "No!" Her tone was harsh, and she hastily tried to soften the refusal. "I mean, thank you—but I don't feel like being in public, exactly."

"I understand. Sometimes in the midst of grief it feels good to have something else to concentrate on, and sometimes it's more comfortable to be alone."

He could say that again, Synnamon thought. Except she was morally certain Conner's definition of alone didn't mean *solitary*, just *private*. If he had the vaguest understanding of her desire to be completely by herself, he wouldn't insist on going to Phoenix, would he? And he'd know that her wish to stay at home tonight instead of going out wasn't entirely on the Contessa's account, but was partly because she didn't feel up to explaining to every friend they ran into that yes, they had reconciled....

She growled as she put the phone down. She'd just have to make it clear over dinner that he wasn't invited to Phoenix, that was all, without letting him realize that she was desperate for a couple of days alone. Though exactly how she was going to convince him...

You might as well argue with an influenza germ, Morea had said.

Hoping that Morea might have some wisdom, Synnamon called the law office to leave a message. "You're actually in?" she said when Morea's secretary put her straight through. "And not busy?"

"I wouldn't go that far," Morea said. "You got through because you're on the list of people I need to call today, anyway. I'm doing my part for the Have a Heart Club, working on the Valentine's Ball. So if you want to buy tickets—"

"Not particularly."

"It's all in a good cause. Of course, I'm sort of glad you put off the purchase till now."

"Why?"

"Because last week you could have gotten by with one ticket, and this week you'll have to buy two. Which makes a cool thousand bucks for the organ transplant program."

Synnamon groaned. "So send me two tickets and I'll write a check. Just don't expect me to show up for the dance."

"Why on earth not? Valentine's Day is for lovers, and—"

"Make that one ticket. Conner can buy his own."

Morea made a sympathetic clucking noise. "But now that you're back together and acting like a pair of cooing doves—"

"Where did you get *that* idea?"

"Overheard it at the Pinnacle last night."

"Since when did the grapevine work that fast?"

"Apparently the diner in question was coming through the hotel lobby downstairs on his way to the restaurant just as Conner was checking out, overheard the address where his luggage was being sent and assumed the rest. Unless you *have* been acting like doves?"

"Certainly not in public. Maybe I won't buy any tickets at all."

"Be a sport, Synnamon. Have a heart, as the organizers would say. At least one ticket—"

"All right, one. No, on second thought, send me two."

"Will you make up your mind?"

"Definitely two," Synnamon said. "That way I can bury them in my lingerie drawer and forget all about the ball. If I don't buy two, you'll call Conner, and he'd not only spring for a pair of tickets, he'd want to go."

"Maybe I should call him anyway," Morea mused. "I might end up with another thousand for the cause."

"And one less friend and client."

"You mean you *are* still my client? In that case, it's a good thing I haven't obeyed Conner's orders to send a bill for my services and cancel you out of my computer."

"A very good thing. I'm trying my best to apply your advice, Morea—"

"Now that's a first," Morea muttered.

Synnamon ignored her. "And be the most flexible and cooperative of wives, so Conner will get tired of the whole thing."

"And how's it working out?"

"It's driving me crazy, and he hasn't even noticed."

"Are you sure he hasn't noticed? Maybe he's trying to

be the most flexible and cooperative of husbands with the specific intention of driving you crazy.''

''If that's what he's doing,'' Synnamon said glumly, ''it's working. And if that's the best suggestion you can give me—''

She heard the door bell chime, and Mrs. Ogden's footsteps faded away down the hall toward the foyer.

''At the moment it is,'' Morea said. ''Frankly, darling, in my experience, you two are breaking virgin ground where divorce is concerned.''

''Oh, that's reassuring.''

''But if you decide to give up the making nice, I can always file an injunction to get him thrown out of the apartment.''

''And wouldn't that look great in court?'' Synnamon muttered. ''He hasn't laid a hand on me. No verbal assaults, not even an implied insult.''

''Mental cruelty,'' Morea said helpfully. ''Playing games with your mind.''

Mrs. Ogden cleared her throat, and Synnamon turned to face her. The housekeeper was standing in the doorway, a long florist's box in her arms. ''Excuse me, but you've got a visitor, Mrs. Welles.''

''All right, thanks.'' The housekeeper went into the kitchen, and Synnamon uncupped her hand from the telephone. ''Morea, this effort to be cheerful and cooperative is wearing on me. I don't know if it's the stress of having Conner around all the time or my howling hormones, but—''

''Personally, I'd bet on the stress. But then,'' Morea mused, ''I don't know anything about the other, so—''

''But if it keeps up, I'm going to have to check myself into a clinic. That, or just turn into a roaring werewolf.''

''Well, maybe that's the answer. Give Conner one long

look at the real, honest you, and he might take to his heels.''

"Screaming all the way? I couldn't be so lucky. Stick to the law, Morea. Your psychological advice seems to lack a little reality, somehow.''

"You asked,'' Morea said cheerfully. "I'll send the tickets over this morning by special messenger.''

"Just in case I'm in the asylum by afternoon?''

"Well, when there's a thousand dollars at stake, it does pay to be careful of these things. Not that I have any real doubts about your sanity, of course.''

"That,'' Synnamon said wryly, "makes one of us. While you're at it, send an extra book of tickets. I'll make a few phone calls myself and see if I can sell them.''

"Thanks, darling. It *is* a good cause, after all.''

"Besides, misery loves company,'' Synnamon finished. "If I have to go to this dance, maybe I can at least cajole all my friends into going, too.''

Mrs. Ogden had gone to the kitchen, so Synnamon couldn't ask who her visitor was. She was startled, therefore, when she looked into the big living room and saw Nicole Fox seated on the edge of a chair.

Nicole jumped up the instant she saw Synnamon. "I didn't mean to intrude this morning,'' she said hastily. "I just brought some flowers by as a thank-you gift for last night, and when I asked about you—''

"Mrs. Ogden practically dragged you in,'' Synnamon added, "and abandoned you before you could say you were only asking in order to be polite.''

Nicole nodded. "Something like that,'' she admitted. "She took the flowers and went that way before I could tell her…'' She took a deep breath. "It's not that I didn't want to see you, but I didn't intend to barge in like this.''

She looked unusually pale, Synnamon thought. She was

a little surprised at the sympathy that trickled through her. The young woman was courageous, that was sure. Nicole could have had the florist make a delivery. What had made her brave the personal contact?

Nicole took two steps toward the door.

It would have been very easy for Synnamon to stand still and do nothing, and in a couple of minutes the woman would be gone. But she couldn't help feeling curious.

"Then you *did* want to see me?" Synnamon asked. Did Nicole intend to ask for Conner's freedom, perhaps? Well, if it was anything like that, they might as well get it out in the open. "Sit down, please. I'll ask Mrs. Ogden to make coffee."

"Oh, no—don't bother with coffee. I don't want to put you to any trouble." Nicole perched on the edge of a chair. "I hope you'll like the flowers as much as I enjoyed myself last night."

"It's very kind of you to bring them yourself," Synnamon said.

"You know, you're not at all..." Nicole's voice trailed off, and a tinge of color crept into her cheeks.

"What you expected," Synnamon said flatly.

"Well, no. Conner told me, you see—"

Synnamon could almost imagine *that* conversation. Didn't a wandering husband always have a tale of woe about his wife, a tale guaranteed to win sympathy from the other woman? Surely Nicole wasn't naive enough to repeat it to her. And why had she been dim-witted enough to invite Nicole to sit down and discuss it, anyway?

"He said that you were practically raised by somebody who was even more a stickler on good behavior than Emily Post," Nicole said. "So of course I thought—"

"That I'd be overbearing and rude to anyone who might not be as knowledgeable?" But Synnamon's mind was only half on the question. That was unusual, for Conner to be talking to Nicole about the Contessa. Of course, he'd cared for her, too. Perhaps, in his grief, he'd turned to Nicole for comfort. "I think Conner overstated the case, however. The Contessa was certainly concerned about proper behavior, but she never criticized anyone else's manners. It's extremely impolite to notice anyone else's bad behavior, she always said."

Nicole considered that and smiled. "It does make sense, doesn't it? But Conner didn't ever say anything negative about her. I'm sorry if I made it sound as if he had. He obviously respected her very much."

Synnamon looked straight at her. "And you're very fond of him, aren't you, to defend him like that to me?"

"Oh, yes." Nicole toyed with the cording on the wing chair she sat in and sighed. "He's—wonderful, that's all. I wish…"

Her eyes were so dilated and full of tears that Synnamon was sure Nicole could no longer see her. And there was a tremor in the woman's voice that expressed her feelings for Conner more convincingly than actual words of love could. The combination left Synnamon feeling as if there was a boulder lodged at the base of her throat.

"You're a very lucky woman," Nicole went on, in a low voice that was next door to tears, "to have him. And now your baby, too."

And how, Synnamon thought helplessly, *would the Contessa have answered that*? "Thank you," she said crisply.

Nicole stood up. "I must go. I'm due at work soon— we're doing some around-the-clock tests, and I'm taking the late shift so I can spend some time at Sherwood, as well. And since I'm sort of leaving the company in the lurch by changing jobs in a busy season—'' She paused. ''But I'm babbling, and you don't want to hear the details. Thanks again for having me over last night. It really opened my eyes...'' Her voice dropped almost to a whisper, so soft that Synnamon wondered if she knew she was speaking aloud. ''About everything I'm missing.''

Synnamon showed her out, then closed the door and leaned against it.

So, in Nicole's opinion, she was a lucky woman. The very thought made her feel hollow.

She wondered what Nicole would have said if she'd announced she'd happily give Conner back to her, wrapped up in hearts-and-flowers gift paper...if only she could.

Conner came home on the dot of six, and a little later, over Mrs. Ogden's chicken Angelique, Synnamon braced herself to bring up the Phoenix trip. She'd rehearsed her little speech in front of her mirror off and on all afternoon, and she was as ready as she could ever be.

The Contessa had asked her to go alone, she'd tell him, so the secluded spot she'd chosen would always remain secret.

The question was whether Conner would fall for the excuse. Or if, at least, he'd pretend to agree, and let her go to Phoenix by herself. She had to admit to having her doubts. Morea might well have a point. If Synnamon could think up this game, so could Conner—and they could no doubt play it with equal facility.

She couldn't quite see what Conner had to gain from the stunt, though, unless he was hoping to make her so tired of him that she'd give up their child into his care and disappear. But of course he needn't have any such elaborate plan as that in mind. It was nothing new, Morea said, for a divorcing couple to try to wear on each others' nerves, for no other reason than just to prove they *could*.

Synnamon only hoped she was being half as successful at driving Conner nuts as he was at making her feel crazy.

She raised a forkful of chicken Angelique to her lips and said, "Conner—"

At the same moment, he said, "I talked to Luigi today."

She was interested despite herself. And also, she admitted, just a little glad for the excuse to put off broaching what was likely to be an uncomfortable discussion. "Did you get him soothed down?"

Conner shook his head. "Not as well as I'd hoped."

"What's the problem?"

"He seems to be convinced I'm going to run the company into the ground without you there to oversee my actions."

"Oh, for heaven's sake." Synnamon's voice was full of disgust. "I've never heard anything so silly."

He looked at her for a long moment, his eyes dark and intense in the dancing light of the candle flames.

Synnamon felt as if he was staring straight through her, and her hands began to shake.

"Thank you for the compliment," he said softly.

Her trembling fingers steadied, and embarrassed warmth rose from the pit of her stomach and suffused her entire body. She hadn't intended to flatter him—she'd only been telling the truth. But it was an odd, uncomfortable feeling to find praise for him rising so automatically to her tongue—without even considering what she wanted to say or the effect it might have.

"At any rate," Conner went on, "I think I need to see him in person."

"And as soon as possible," Synnamon agreed. "Where

Luigi is concerned, it's important to control the damage before it gets worse.''

''Exactly. I'm glad your assessment of the situation agrees with mine. I've made arrangements to visit him this weekend.''

Instead of going to Phoenix. Now Synnamon was glad she hadn't rushed into the discussion. He'd handed her a trump card, and if she played it carefully... ''I understand,'' she said quickly. ''Sherwood's concerns come first, and you must do whatever you feel is necessary for the business.'' She looked at her plate and then gave him the most sincerely troubled look she could manage. ''I do want to go to Phoenix, though, Conner. I don't want to put the trip off any longer. So if you don't mind, while you're off seeing Luigi—''

''Of course,'' Conner said. ''Carol already has tickets for us both on the Friday afternoon Denver to Phoenix flight.''

Us? ''But...'' She stopped and tried again. ''I thought you said you need to see Luigi right away.''

Conner nodded. ''That's what makes it perfect. Luigi's spending the winter in his house in Scottsdale—right next door to Phoenix.'' He cut another bite of chicken Angelique. ''Which means we have a wonderful excuse to be in his neighborhood—and also that you can help convince him Sherwood is in good hands.''

The Contessa's villa looked just the same. Synnamon got out of the rental car and stood for a moment staring at the quiet facade of the house. It took no imagination at all to picture the Contessa at ease on the chaise longue in her morning room, basking in the soft, filtered sunshine she favored and waiting for them to arrive. There would be hugs and happy greetings, followed by excellent coffee—

or more probably sherry, since it was already cocktail hour—and some of Mrs. Hartford's gourmet snacks, and delightful conversation....

Synnamon sighed and let her shoulders slump. Conner, who was lifting luggage from the trunk of the car, turned his head quickly to look at her. She said quietly, "The Contessa always called this the city of new beginnings— but I had no idea how difficult this would be."

The front door opened and Hartford bustled out to help with the luggage. Over Conner's protests, he gathered up the two largest pieces and smiled tentatively at Synnamon. "Welcome home, Mrs. Welles."

She closed her eyes in pain. She didn't want to think of this as her home instead of the Contessa's. Then she squared her shoulders and picked up a flight bag.

Conner took it out of her hand. "I told you not to carry things."

"I'm only trying to make myself useful," she muttered.

"So you don't have to think about the Contessa? This is the hardest part, Synnamon—going in the first time without her being there. Get that behind you and you'll be all right. Remember going into your father's penthouse right after he died?"

She nodded. "It's different, though," she said, almost under her breath.

"A little, perhaps. But after this first time, it will never be quite as difficult again."

It was a *lot* different, she wanted to say. She had mourned Silas Sherwood, of course, but even more she had grieved the father she'd have liked to have—a father who thought she was special, who wanted to spend time with her. And because Silas hadn't been the sort of father she'd longed for, she had to admit—even though she was a bit ashamed of the fact—that there had been a little relief mixed in with her shock and sadness. Relief that the life-long effort to please him was over at last.

The villa smelled of something spicy. But there was another scent, too—the almost-stale aroma of a room that had been closed up too long. It seemed more like a photograph than a real room, Synnamon thought, as if the image of a single instant had been captured and frozen, never to recur. There was no dust, of course, but there was also no air of human occupation. Each dainty pillow sat squarely in place as if a body had never leaned against it. The piano's music rack was empty, the strings silent. And for the first time in all the years she had known this room, there were no fresh flowers anywhere.

The lack of roses brought home the Contessa's absence as nothing else could have. Tears welled in Synnamon's eyes and overflowed. She tried to control them, turning her back in the hope that Conner wouldn't see, but the effort was futile.

He said something under his breath that she didn't quite catch and came across the room to her.

Synnamon willed herself not to tense, but he didn't touch her, just pulled a white handkerchief from his pocket and put it in her hand.

"I apologize for offending you with my expressions of grief," she said. She knew her tone was just short of nasty, and at the moment she didn't care.

Conner's voice was calm. "Feeling sorry about the Contessa is one thing. Feeling sorry for yourself is another. Which is this?"

I hate it, Synnamon thought, *when he's so logical—and so right.* "The least you could do is let me take it out on you," she grumbled. "I'd feel ever so much better."

The corner of his mouth turned up slightly. "No doubt. What did it, anyway? I can't see anything different."

"The roses," she said. "The Contessa always had roses." She mopped at her eyes.

"Don't—you'll smear your mascara." Conner took the handkerchief out of her hand.

"No, I won't. It's your new nonstreaking kind."

"Well, nothing's guaranteed if you scrub at it like that." He touched the folded edge of the handkerchief gently to her swollen eyelids. "Would you feel better if there were roses?"

Synnamon considered. "I don't think so. That would just be pretending."

"Then we won't have roses. Perhaps— Oh, here comes Hartford, and I smell coffee."

Coffee, she thought. Not sherry. "Did you tell him I'm not drinking alcohol these days?"

Conner looked thoughtful. "No. I thought you might have. Or perhaps he's a mind reader. Are you, Hartford?"

"A mind reader, sir? Not at all. But Mrs. Hartford made gingersnaps this afternoon, and she thought coffee would go better. But if you'd prefer a Scotch and water—"

"No. The coffee will be fine. We've made a dinner date for tomorrow, by the way, so would you tell Mrs. Hartford she doesn't need to worry about feeding us?"

"With Luigi?" Synnamon asked.

Conner nodded. "At his estate, no less." He poured cream into his cup and added, "You look disappointed, Hartford."

"My wife will be, sir. She's been looking forward to a couple of healthy appetites. I must say I sympathize. Life is a bit dull now."

"I'd think you'd enjoy the peace and quiet," Conner said.

"But we feel so unnecessary, sir. In fact, we'd hoped to talk to you both about that very thing."

"Sit down," Conner said.

Hartford didn't seem to hear the invitation. "We thought, perhaps, if you could use us in Denver..."

Conner looked thoughtful.

The silence drew out uncomfortably till Synnamon could stand it no longer. "I'm sorry, but you know it's not a terribly large apartment, and Mrs. Ogden is already in place. I'm afraid no one would be very happy, all tripping over one another. And there is only a single room and bath, not even a butler's suite—"

Conner interrupted. "However, we may buy a house before long. With the baby coming, we could really use the space. And once we make the move—"

"A baby? What wonderful news! Wait till I tell Mrs. Hartford. She'll be thrilled." Hartford's smile faded. "I only wish the Contessa could have known."

After he had hurried toward the kitchen, Synnamon eyed Conner with distaste. "You had to tell him, didn't you?"

"About the baby? That isn't the sort of secret one can keep indefinitely. And we could use more space than we have in the apartment."

"Well, that's certainly true enough. We could *use* the entire planet of Mars. You can have the top hemisphere, I'll take the bottom." She saw the quizzical quirk of his eyebrows and thought better of the outburst. "You must admit, Conner, that it would be polite to tell me these things before you start making announcements to the butler."

"You're right, of course, though the notion actually hadn't occurred to me till right at that moment. But since you think it's a good idea, too—"

Mrs. Hartford bustled in. "How delightful! A baby... And Hartford tells me we're coming to Denver, too."

Synnamon gave up and sipped her coffee. She couldn't possibly fight them all—at least, not just now, when the only thing she felt was overwhelmingly tired.

"I think," she said, "I'll go up for a nap." She pushed her cup away.

"You must take care of yourself," Mrs. Hartford said. As Synnamon left the living room, she heard the housekeeper exclaiming, "Of course you'll want a boy first, Mr. Welles. Every man thinks in terms of a son first, I think."

"Perhaps you're right," Conner said. His voice was slow, lazy, almost dreamy. "A son."

Of course, Synnamon thought. *First, last and always, no doubt*. And if the baby was a girl instead, just how disappointed would he be?

The guest room had been rearranged since their last visit, and instead of the primly separated twin beds it was once more a king-size rectangle. Synnamon shook her head and considered calling Hartford upstairs and asking him to change it. But it seemed like far too much effort—not only for him to do the work, but even for her to make the request.

Besides, if she asked to have the beds rearranged—or if she used the Contessa's boudoir instead and left Conner in the guest room—she might as well announce that the supposedly fairy-tale marriage had hit the shoals some time ago. That was hardly something she wanted to do now that the Hartfords knew about the baby.

And what was the point, after all? Two months ago, the beds had been separated by the width of the room, but it hadn't prevented her from making a mistake that would resonate through the rest of her days.

The biggest mistake, she told herself grimly, of a lifetime.

CHAPTER EIGHT

"THERE'S Luigi's house," Synnamon said. "At least, the number on the gatepost matches what's written in your notebook."

The rental car pulled slowly between the gates and paused at the end of the drive as if Conner was hesitant to go any closer. "*That's* what you call a house?"

"In polite company, yes."

He cast a curious glance at her. "The Contessa's philosophy sank in deep, didn't it?"

"You're surprised?"

"By you, no. By the house—yes, a bit. I expected grandiosity from Luigi. A Roman style villa, perhaps. But I must say the minaret atop the chalet roof is just a little more than I was prepared for."

Synnamon glanced at his notebook, still open in her lap, and said hopefully, "I don't suppose Luigi could have given you the wrong house number?"

"No. And I'm afraid I didn't turn the digits around when I wrote them down, either." The car edged forward.

"I didn't think so. Actually, I'm not at all surprised. It's exactly the sort of thing Harold Henderson would think up."

"Who's Harold Henderson?"

"Luigi." She looked at him in surprise. Conner was still staring at the house, his hands lying loose on the steering wheel. The shadowed light cast by the gatepost lamps cut his face into sharp angles. "Didn't my father ever tell you about him? He's about as Italian as pizza."

134

Conner frowned. "Wasn't pizza invented in Chicago?"

"Or New York City, at the moment I can't remember which. But it surely wasn't Rome, and that's my point. Luigi was invented—for lack of a better term—in the south Bronx. I can't believe my father never told you."

"Perhaps Silas was keeping a few secrets back to maintain his value to the company," Conner mused.

"I wouldn't put it past him."

"Do you realize," Conner went on, "that you never refer to Silas as anything but 'my father'?"

She shot a sideways look at him, but he was staring straight ahead. "Really?" Synnamon kept her tone polite but flat.

"It's very interesting. Even to his face, I never heard you say 'Dad' or 'Papa' or even 'Father'."

She deliberately widened her eyes, feigning shock. "How about 'Daddy, darling'?"

"Don't try to be flippant. You know perfectly well you've never—at least in my hearing—called him anything of the sort."

"Well, you knew my father. It shouldn't be too hard to figure out." She closed his pocket notebook and held it out. "Here—you'd no doubt be lost without this."

"Possibly. And Carol would be devastated if she had to start from scratch." His palm brushed the back of her hand as he took the small leather book. The contact sent a shiver up Synnamon's arm, but Conner didn't seem to notice. He tucked the book into his breast pocket, parked the car in the enormous concrete circle in front of the house and reached for the door handle. Then he settled into his seat with a frown.

"On second thought," he said, "is this a parking lot or a sculpture garden? I don't see any evidence of cars, and there's the strangest piece of metal I've ever seen planted right in the middle.''

"I'm willing to take my chances. If Luigi gets offended and throws us out, we can go to Emilio's for a hamburger.''

Conner came around the car. "Where's that?''

"It's a little dive in a very bad neighborhood—but the food is ambrosia. The Contessa used to take me there.''

"The Contessa was quite the woman, wasn't she?'' His tone was admiring.

Synnamon had to clear her throat. "I always thought so. You know, a lot of people expected her to be a snob, but she was a genuine lady. She probably wouldn't even have winced at Luigi's minarets.''

"Now that,'' Conner muttered, "would be a challenge.'' He tucked her hand into the bend of his elbow.

Luigi himself came to greet them in the entrance hall.

Synnamon could feel Conner's muscles trembling under her fingertips. Not from nervousness, though, she was positive of that. She wouldn't be surprised if it was repressed laughter that was causing those tremors. And she had to admit that Luigi was a sight to behold.

The shiny wallpaper—pure gold leaf, Synnamon was sure—reflected the light from the dozen torch-shaped sconces and made his hair look like polished amber. The shiny gold tunic he wore was a cross between a toga and Hollywood's idea of an Arab chieftain's robe, and he bowed ceremonially from the waist as he greeted them.

Black, beady eyes flickered over Conner and came to rest approvingly on Synnamon. "My dear,'' he said. "You're as sinfully lovely as ever. Silas was right—he told me once that you'd mature beautifully.''

"No doubt he added that it would be entirely due to constant use of Sherwood cosmetics,'' Synnamon said.

"But of course—our Silas was a man who was proud of his product. Conner, I don't believe we've met except over the telephone, have we? What a happy occasion this is, then. I'm glad you made the effort to come all this way just to see me."

The small black eyes had sharpened, Synnamon saw, as if he was calculating his worth to the Sherwood corporation. If two senior officers and shareholders gave up an entire weekend to placate him...

She gave a tiny shake of her head. "I'm sorry to disappoint you, Luigi, but we had some family business here, as well."

"Of course," he murmured. "But I shouldn't keep you standing here. Come in, come in."

The lounge to which he led them managed to make the front entrance look underdecorated. Every wall was draped with rich brocade, and the folds of heavy fabric stirred uneasily with every movement. The room, Synnamon thought, was positively creepy—as if there were secret listeners behind every panel.

She turned down a poisonous-looking cocktail offered by a young woman wearing a skimpy uniform, which looked more like a costume, and asked for club soda with a twist of lime.

Luigi frowned. "Just club soda? I'm sure my staff could find anything you'd like."

"Not right now, thanks."

Conner looked up from a dubious appraisal of his glass. "We're expecting a child later in the year, so of course Synnamon is watching very carefully what she eats and drinks."

"I see," Luigi said. "So the Sherwood empire will be in safe hands for another generation? A fine, strong boy to fill Silas's shoes?"

"We certainly hope so," Conner agreed. "Don't we, darling?"

Synnamon forced herself to nod and look as enthusiastic as she could manage.

Luigi monopolized the conversation all the way through dinner, talking of his chain of spas and the new beauty treatments he was introducing. Synnamon listened with half an ear. She was trying to figure out the contents of her entree and wishing she could send it to Sherwood's lab for analysis before she risked another bite. She didn't realize how far her mind had wandered until Luigi said, "Perhaps after dinner I can show you, Synnamon."

Her gaze flew from her plate to Conner's face, trying to telegraph her panic. Surely he wouldn't ignore her plight. He simply had to rescue her or risk the outcome of the entire evening. But his expression was smoothly noncommittal—or was that the most infinitesimal nod she'd ever seen? She hated to bet on it, but she had no other choice.

"That would be lovely, Luigi," she managed. "And Conner, too, of course?"

"Of course," Luigi said smoothly. "Are you finished, my dear? Didn't you like my chef's creation?"

"It was excellent. But I have a very small appetite these days."

"Then let's go back to the lounge for our coffee and dessert." Luigi tossed down his napkin and led the way. "Take this chair, my dear," he told Synnamon, indicating a long chaise. "It'll make your massage easier."

He strolled across to a drapery panel, which looked no different than the others, pulled it aside and pressed a button on a huge control panel.

"Massage?" Synnamon asked under her breath.

Conner shrugged. "You agreed to it."

Synnamon had to take a deep breath, count to a hundred and remind herself that kicking was forbidden—no matter how much he deserved it.

The same scantily clad young woman who had served drinks came in with a silver tray that contained something that would have looked more at home in an emergency room. Luigi intercepted Synnamon's look and said, as he picked it up, "A wonderful new development, I think. This is the only silicone gel face mask that exists. It allows us to do facial massage without disturbing the client's makeup. Fingers alone are so untidy, don't you think?" He advanced on her. "If you'll just lean back and let me drape this over your face—"

She shot a look at Conner.

With deceptive ease, he moved into position at the head of her chaise. "Why don't you show me the techniques, Luigi?"

Luigi smiled. "Very well. But without the mask, you can't reproduce the results. And the mask is going to be exclusively available at Luigi Salons."

"Of course," Conner said genially. "But if you were to allow us to manufacture them for you…"

"That remains to be seen." Luigi draped the gel envelope over Synnamon's face. "Put your fingertips right here. Now press gently and draw them upward, like so." He nodded. "That's it."

The pressure of Conner's hands against her face was almost nonexistent, but the silicone mask seemed to magnify the effect, sending tiny surges of energy through each muscle.

"Have you already made arrangements with another manufacturer?" Conner asked.

"Not just yet. But I must be honest. I don't like what

I see going on at Sherwood these days. The contamination in the manufacturing plant, for instance—''

''That could have happened anywhere,'' Synnamon tried to say. But the words came out garbled, and for a split-second Conner's fingertips pressed against her jaw-line on both sides of her chin. Not a very subtle way to tell her to keep her mouth shut, Synnamon thought—but it was effective. She sank a little deeper into the lounge.

''I understand your concern,'' Conner said. ''We knew we were taking a risk, Synnamon and I, by announcing what was going on. I think most of our competition would have tried to hide the fact—but we had faith in our customers. We knew they'd understand the situation and would appreciate our honesty.''

Luigi sniffed. ''That's just a fancy-dress way of saying that you *couldn't* keep it secret. In Silas's day, things like that wouldn't have happened.''

''Oh, no—they happened. He just managed to keep the news away from the customers. You're right about one thing, Luigi. I'm not Silas.''

Conner's fingers didn't stop moving in soft patterns over Synnamon's face, and despite her intense interest in the conversation going on over her head, she couldn't stop herself from surrendering to the gentleness of his touch.

It was odd, though. Her face was relaxing under the soft stroking pressure, the tenseness in her temples was gone, and her cheek muscles felt as soft as butter under a summer sun. But instead of vanishing altogether, the tension felt as if it had sunk deep inside her body. Far from the sensitive touch of his fingertips, there seemed to be a coiled spring, and it was winding tighter with every stroke of his hands.

''I don't have anything against you, exactly,'' Luigi

said. "But when an old family firm goes out of the family, something's lost."

"But Sherwood hasn't gone out of the family," Conner pointed out.

"Technically, no. But it's not like you were Silas's son. And with Synnamon leaving—"

"Who said she's leaving?" Conner's voice held a note of mild curiosity.

Synnamon almost sat up straight in shock, but his fingertips pressed her into the soft lounge.

"She's chosen for the moment to concentrate on a healthy baby," Conner went on, "but that doesn't mean she's less interested in Sherwood just because she's not holding down a day-to-day job there. In fact, she may take more real interest in policy-making now that she can focus on the big picture instead of the details of servicing customer accounts."

Very smooth, Synnamon thought. She almost believed him herself. Though maybe he was completely serious. He hadn't said anything about taking her advice, just that she'd have more time to offer it.

"Besides," Conner mused, "who knows? Maybe once the baby's born Synnamon will decide to run Sherwood all by herself, and I'll stay home and raise him."

"Very funny," Luigi said, grunting. "But of course we'll have to wait and see what happens when the time comes, won't we? For right now, I just want you to know I'm keeping a close eye on things. And if I see one more piece of evidence that Sherwood is falling short of Silas's standards, you won't get another chance to sweet-talk me—either one of you."

For a moment, Synnamon thought she could detect in the blunt tones the last traces of a Bronx accent. Then Luigi's voice regained its usual oily charm. "And if

Synnamon decides to throw you out altogether, Conner, I'd be happy to take you on.''

Conner's fingers slipped, and a corner of his fingernail jabbed Synnamon's face under the edge of the mask. It wasn't a scratch. If she hadn't been so sensitized by the massage, she might not have felt it. And she understood why he'd slipped. She'd been a bit stunned herself by the idea that Luigi wanted to hire him.

"I'd say you're a natural at facial massage," Luigi went on easily, "and I know a lot of ladies who'd be happy to let you practice on them."

As soon as she thought she could get by with it, Synnamon pleaded exhaustion. It wasn't entirely a ploy, either—she *was* dead tired. But she was also horribly keyed up. Even after she'd sat up and taken the mask off, the effects of the massage lingered. She could still feel not only the soft stroking of Conner's fingertips but the tension that had retreated inward, tension that refused to go away.

Once safely out of Luigi's driveway, she put her head back against the seat of the rental car and said, "That was pretty smooth, Conner."

"Likewise. I couldn't have pulled it off without you."

She didn't believe that for a moment, but she didn't feel like arguing. "How long do you think you can keep him believing that I'll be back to work before long?"

"You might want to return."

"To what? Annie's doing fine."

Conner shrugged. "There are other jobs."

"I don't think so." She sat up. "I'm starving. Do you think Mrs. Hartford would mind if we raided the refrigerator?"

"Mind? I think she'd be more likely to empty it for

you. But I thought you told Luigi you had a very small appetite these days.''

"Only where unidentified food is concerned. What *was* that main dish, anyway?''

"I don't think you want to know.''

"In that case, don't tell me.''

The corner of his mouth quirked. "What was that place you were telling me about? The dive with the great burgers?''

"Emilio's?''

"That's it. Let's go there. I could stand a thick, hot, all-American cheeseburger right now.''

Synnamon hesitated. Surely there wasn't any reason not to go. Besides, the alternative was to return to the Contessa's, invade the refrigerator and sooner or later retreat to that shared king-size bed. The longer she could put that off, the better she'd feel. "All right. Head toward downtown, and I'll give you directions when we get close.''

Emilio's was even more of a dive than on her last visit. Though it was clean, the decor ran to vinyl, paper and sturdy glass, and there were even more neon signs in the windows and above the bar than Synnamon remembered. The jukebox was playing, and two couples occupied the tiny dance floor. But despite the hour, only one of the high-backed booths was empty, and without waiting to be noticed by the waitress, Synnamon led the way to it.

Conner slid into the seat across from her and looked around. "The Contessa actually came here?''

"Not only did she come, but Emilio would cook her hamburgers himself and keep her up to date on the doings of all his various nieces and nephews. I got the sweetest note from him after she died—complete with grease stains.''

The waitress set a half-sheet of paper in front of each of them.

Synnamon glanced at the smeared photocopy and looked up in surprise. "A menu? What's Emilio's coming to?"

The waitress shrugged. "Some of the tourists get nervous without one. What can I get you?"

"Hot tea, please. And I'll have a medium burger with everything."

Conner didn't even look at his menu. "I'll take your word for it. The same for me, but with coffee."

"I don't mind if you have a beer or something, Conner. Just because I'm being careful what I drink these days—"

He shook his head. "No, that concoction at Luigi's was enough to put me off alcohol for life. I don't know what was in it, but it tasted like the inside of a bat cave."

The waitress returned with their drinks, and Synnamon toyed with her spoon while she waited for her tea to brew. It felt odd, being out with him like this. Almost as if it was a first date.

In fact, she thought, she hadn't been this anxious on their first date. Of course, that evening more than a year ago had been a company function, and they'd only gone together at Silas's suggestion—so Synnamon hadn't really looked at it as a date at all. It was only later that she realized the quiet young man in the long white lab coat was paying a great deal more attention to her than she had expected him to.

She looked up from her tea and found his attention focused on her, his eyes intent and thoughtful. There were two tiny frown marks between his eyebrows, she noted. For the first time she realized that there were other lines in his face, as well. Were they new, or had she just never noticed them before?

She was chastened by the knowledge that it had been a long time since she had really looked at him—at the chiseled face, the strong, lean body, the graceful hands. So long, in fact, that in a way he hardly looked familiar at all.

And what was he thinking as he looked at her?

There was an odd twinge in the pit of her stomach as she wondered what he was feeling. Curiosity, perhaps, at how they had come to this pass. Sadness, no doubt. And probably regret.

Nervously, she raised a hand to brush her cheek. "I was so frazzled that I forgot to ask. *Did* Luigi's mask make a mess of my makeup?"

For a moment she thought he hadn't heard. Then, slowly, he shook his head. "No, it performed as promised. You look fine."

"Good." She folded her hands around her teacup. "It was quite a sensation. Are you serious about wanting to manufacture it?"

He shrugged. "We'd have to look at the details, of course. Making a few for Luigi's spas probably wouldn't be profitable."

"He might consent to a home version."

"If you feel like trying to persuade him, go right ahead. Synnamon—"

There was a firmness about his tone as he said her name that Synnamon hadn't heard for a while—not since those first arguments about the baby—and a shiver ran through her at the reminder.

Conner looked at the table while he drew a rectangle with the base of his coffee mug. "I know you want your privacy tomorrow when you go to scatter the Contessa's ashes, and I respect that. I'll stay as far away as you like—even if it's here in Phoenix while you go out in the desert.

But is there any chance you'd reconsider? I'd like to go with you.''

She didn't answer.

A moment later, he said quietly, ''You see, I lost my grandmother when I was a teenager. Nobody told me she was so very sick till she was gone, and then it was too late. I couldn't even go to the funeral. She was very different from the Contessa, of course—and yet the way they loved was so terribly similar.''

''And you need to say goodbye?''

''I'd like to. It's up to you, of course.''

Synnamon hesitated. ''All right. You can come with me, Conner.''

Somehow, the simple phrase didn't feel like an invitation. It felt more like a promise.

Suddenly, a question seemed to echo in her mind. *Why can't we make it work*? she asked herself.

If the baby had come along earlier, before they had started the legal paperwork, they'd have tried to go on, and the idea of a divorce might never have come up at all.

There was Nicole, of course. But perhaps that, too, was partly Synnamon's own fault. In the months they'd lived together, she'd never been suspicious of Conner. He'd given her no reason to wonder if there were other women in his life. And even if that was largely because Sherwood itself seemed more attractive to him than any other woman could possibly be—well, that was a fact of life Synnamon had long ago accepted.

Maybe Conner was right, after all, and they could make it work. He seemed willing enough to give Nicole up. That was clear from the way Nicole herself was acting. And once they'd adjusted to the new realities forced upon them by circumstances, they might rub along fairly comfortably together for the rest of their lives.

There was an all-gone feeling in her chest at the idea. She didn't know whether it came from the necessity of giving up the only bit of independence she'd ever experienced, or from uncertainty about the roles she would be called on to play over the years. The only thing she knew for sure was it would take time to truly get used to the idea of being Conner's wife once more, and the mother of his child.

And after all, she reminded herself, there was no rush. She needn't decide anything right away, for time was the one thing they had in abundance.

"You miss him, don't you?" Morea challenged.

Synnamon hardly heard her. She didn't realize how far her thoughts had wandered while Morea studied the dessert tray. "What did you say?"

Morea shook her head at the waiter, then snapped the last bread stick in two and brandished half of it at Synnamon. "Conner's been gone not quite a week and you're mooning around like a—"

"Please," Synnamon begged. "Spare me the comparisons."

"Then you admit that you miss him?"

Synnamon hesitated. Three weeks ago, when she'd been trying to find an excuse to escape to Phoenix by herself for a couple of days, she'd have found the idea of missing Conner laughable. But now that he'd been in Asia for five days, trying to work out a sudden kink in the supply of product packaging...

"Sort of," Synnamon said.

"And you actually think it's going to be happily ever after?"

"I wouldn't go that far. But Conner's right. We made a deal, and there's no reason we can't live with it. Of course we both wish things were different, but where there's a child, sometimes people have to make sacrifices."

"All right, spare me the sermon. And pardon me if I don't throw out your case file just yet."

"You never throw out case files."

"Of course not—but I'm not usually so certain that I'll need them again." She slipped the bill for their lunch from under Synnamon's hand. "My treat. Consider it a good-luck gift."

"Thanks—I think."

Morea grinned. "But don't lose my phone number. You'll need it when Prince Charming makes you break out in warts after all. I have to go, darling. There are half a dozen clients on my calendar this afternoon."

She swirled off, and Synnamon finished her coffee in peace before she strolled to the Sherwood complex. The weather was pleasant for the end of January—in fact, it almost felt like spring—and it was nice not to feel rushed, as she had for so many years.

Annie was doing just fine in her new job, and there was really nothing for Synnamon to do except provide moral support now and then. The only reason she had even come to work today was that Mrs. Ogden was spring-cleaning the apartment with a vengeance. With a baby on the way, she'd announced, there was serious work to be done.

Though to be honest, it would be more accurate to say that was the main reason, not the only one. For Morea was right. She was missing Conner.

The two weeks since their return from Phoenix hadn't been exactly easy. There had been tense moments. She'd been snappish on occasion, and Conner had seemed moody now and then. But there was a growing peace within Synnamon, a sense that she was doing the right thing. It had started, she thought, out in the desert when she had scattered the Contessa's ashes in the out-of-the-way spot she had loved, and Conner had not said a word to break the mood. She had felt closer to him in that moment than ever before.

Just inside Sherwood's lobby, she stopped in the main ladies' room to repair her lipstick and was startled to catch a glimpse in the mirror of Nicole. Her face looked blotchy, her eyes were red-rimmed, and she was pressing two fingers to the center of her forehead as if she was in pain.

Synnamon couldn't help but feel sympathetic toward Nicole and a little annoyed with Conner. She'd known the job wasn't going to be an easy one for Nicole—or any outsider—to take on. And Synnamon knew that feeling of helpless inadequacy, too—the sense that the job was far too big and her talents far too small. But she'd really thought Nicole could handle it.

She carefully outlined her lips, then said, without looking at the other woman, "Is there anything I can do to help?"

Nicole shook her head. "No. Thanks anyway."

Synnamon twisted her lip brush in the tube and began to fill in the outline she'd made. "If you're having trouble with your staff—"

"No," Nicole said drearily. "It's not the job. Believe me, I wish it was."

"Then are you ill? There's a lot of flu going around."

Nicole sighed. "It's not flu."

"Overwork? You've been holding two jobs."

There was a half-hysterical catch in Nicole's voice.

"You, of all people, should understand what I'm feeling right now."

"Oh, no." Synnamon's voice was barely a breath.

"Yes," Nicole said flatly. "You see, I'm pregnant, too."

CHAPTER NINE

THE best measure of Synnamon's shock, perhaps, was the fact that her first thought was to wonder how the Contessa would have advised handling a problem like this.

It was a thorny etiquette problem, indeed, so ridiculous that it was almost laughable. But one more look at Nicole's ravaged face removed the last hope that this was someone's sick idea of a practical joke.

As the truth sank in, Synnamon found herself clinging to the edge of the sink, trying to stop her knees from shaking.

"How long?" she said. It was an idiotic question, of course—as if it mattered. As if it was any of her business, really.

"A month. Maybe a little more."

"That's so little time. Are you—" She stopped. Of course Nicole was certain. She was levelheaded and professional, not the sort to panic till the facts were in.

"I ran the test myself," Nicole said drearily. "I thought I was all right. Then a little while ago, it just hit me—the enormousness of it all."

"It does that," Synnamon agreed. There was an irony in their similarities, which under other circumstances would have been deliciously funny, she thought. Well, maybe someday she'd have enough distance and detachment to enjoy looking back on it all. But in the meantime...

Synnamon counted back. *A month. Maybe a little more.*

About the time they were in Fargo, she thought. Conner had sounded so happy when he'd called her from Fargo.

Conner.

There was the tiniest bit of comfort in knowing that when he went to Fargo, he hadn't yet known about Synnamon's child. And he hadn't known about Nicole's baby when he announced that he and Synnamon would stick to the vows they'd made.

Synnamon could feel sympathetic about the trap he was going to find himself caught in. Committed to a woman he didn't love because of an accidental pregnancy, while the woman he cared about was also carrying his child.

Almost sympathetic, she thought dryly.

She asked, half-afraid of the answer, "Have you told Conner?"

Nicole shook her head. "Not yet. I can't. He's already so—"

She stopped, leaving Synnamon wondering exactly what she'd intended to say before she'd thought better of it.

Synnamon could think of half a dozen possibilities. *Busy. Upset. Angry. Miserable.* Maybe it didn't even matter which word Nicole would have chosen.

Nicole said, "He's been under so much stress..." Her gaze met Synnamon's, and she gulped. "With this trip, I mean."

"And everything else," Synnamon said bleakly. "I know. Don't worry about hurting *my* feelings. Just the same, he'll have to know."

Nicole nodded. "Of course. But I need to think it through myself first. I only found out for sure this morning." Something close to panic flared in her eyes. "You don't mean to tell him, do you? Synnamon, please—promise you'll let me handle it."

Synnamon wanted to scream. This was hardly a secret she wanted to share, but now that she was in the middle of it, there weren't a lot of options—and all of them were bad ones. She could make the promise Nicole asked for and trust that the woman would carry through. She could tell Conner herself, and let the fallout rain over them all. Or she could pretend she'd never walked into the ladies' room this morning.

Right, she thought. *And while I'm at it, I'll pretend the sky is chartreuse, too.*

She knew better than to give her word. And yet she knew just as clearly that no matter what Nicole did, she herself wouldn't be the one to tell Conner. Synnamon couldn't bring herself to barge into the middle of what should be a sensitive and private and happy moment.

Poor Nicole, she thought. It was nightmare enough, this situation they were all caught in. But if Synnamon was the one to break this news to Conner, it could only get worse. She wouldn't do that to any of them.

"You'll have to tell him soon," she said.

Relief gleamed in Nicole's eyes. "I will. I promise I will. But I need a little time to think first."

Synnamon could understand that. She'd felt the same need herself. *And look at where it got me*, she thought.

Still almost in a daze, she retreated to the little office she'd adopted. It was down the hall from her old one and around a corner, close enough to be handy if Annie needed her, but out of the way otherwise. She'd never been so glad to be away from Sherwood's bustle. She closed the door behind her and sank into her chair.

"How could he do this to me?" she whispered.

The words seemed to echo in the room and in her brain.

How strange it was, she thought, for her to react that way. After all, wasn't this—in a convoluted and painful sort of way—going to bring about exactly what she'd wanted?

There was no question in her mind that Conner would want to be free now. Offered a choice between building a family with a woman he cared about and one he felt only duty toward, there could be no doubt what his choice would be. And that would leave Synnamon with exactly what she wanted—her freedom, her child…and probably no interference at all from Conner.

But that *wasn't* what she wanted.

She stared across the room, not seeing her surroundings as the kaleidoscope in her mind slowly turned, shattering her long-held image of herself and bringing into focus a new and unfamiliar reality.

She didn't want her freedom. She wanted what she had glimpsed in Phoenix, that night in Emilio's bar—a marriage that might not be passionate but was calm and peaceful and caring. A relationship that might not be precisely loving but that included friendship and companionship. A family that took in mother and father and child.

Why don't you stop lying to yourself? she accused. The truth was, she wouldn't begin to be content with that. Even more than she wanted her child, she wanted Conner. His friendship, his passion…his love.

Had her love for him sneaked up on her in the few weeks since they'd made this feeble effort to reconcile? Or had she always loved him and hidden the fact from herself?

She looked hard into the hidden corners of her heart and saw a painful truth that she had been trying for weeks to ignore.

Her pregnancy had been purely accidental. She was not calculating or cruel enough to plan to bring a child into the world to serve as a bargaining chip. But the seduction that night in Phoenix—and it had been a seduction, she admitted now—had not been an accident. On some level, she had been trying to prove that there was still something between them, that Conner still desired her, that it wasn't all over, after all.

She had been trying to win him back because deep inside, she had known even then that she loved him.

Synnamon propped her elbows on the desk blotter and put her face in her hands. Her head throbbed worse with every heartbeat.

She'd thought she'd made the mistake of a lifetime— but she'd been wrong. She knew now that hers had been the mistake of *several* lifetimes. Hers. Conner's. Nicole's. And that of not one but two innocent babies.

And now that the trouble had come to light, what on earth were they going to do about it?

Synnamon didn't expect Conner to come directly to the apartment. His plane was due to land at mid-afternoon, and she thought he'd go to the office.

After more than a week in Asia, his in-basket was over-flowing. Synnamon knew what it looked like because several times in the past few days his secretary had asked her advice on how to handle the more pressing concerns. And Conner had to know what it would look like, too.

But he had come home instead.

Synnamon knew he was there the moment his key clicked in the door, even though she was at the far end of the apartment in her office alcove, too far away to hear the tiny noise.

He's home, her heart sang. *He came straight home*!

Then the still-sane part of her brain kicked into gear, reminding her that he might live here for a few more days, but it was not his home now, and it would never be again. All she could do was to treasure those last few days.

Or maybe it wouldn't be days. Perhaps he had come straight to the apartment to tell her that he'd talked to Nicole already. Maybe in a matter of minutes he'd break the news to Synnamon that it was all over.

And she would have to hold up her head and smile, and try not to gasp for breath as if she'd just finished a marathon.

She hadn't seen Nicole since they'd parted in the ladies' room four days ago. But Conner's secretary had his itinerary. If Nicole had braced herself to tell him, all she'd have had to do was make an excuse about why she needed to call.

Synnamon could almost feel his footsteps coming closer down the carpeted hall. It was funny, she thought, how quickly she had become sensitized to his presence—and how long it had taken her to become fully aware of it. That fact alone should have warned her that she wasn't indifferent to him, after all. If she'd only had enough brain to wonder why she felt that way...

Conner had shed his jacket and slung it over his shoulder, and he was loosening his tie when he appeared in the doorway of her office.

Synnamon put down the telephone, checked another name off Morea's list of possible Valentine's Ball ticket buyers, and looked at him.

Trying to appear pleasant but unexcited at the sight was one of the hardest things she had ever done. Just looking at him sent tiny darts of painful pleasure through her body. She'd never seen him in quite this way before, with the knowledge that she loved him coloring her vision.

He looked tired. The lines in his face were deeper, and

there was a blue shadow under his eyes, so faint that only her newly sensitized gaze could have picked it up.

She wanted to reach up to him, to stroke the lines away, to hold him and force him to rest.

"Hi," he said. "I thought maybe you'd be at Sherwood today."

The low voice reached straight through Synnamon and twisted her heart. She had to force herself to look away and shrug. "I didn't feel like it. I've been in most days."

"I know. Carol told me you'd helped out with some details."

She tensed. "Carol asked for help, so I did what I could. That's all."

"You're a bit touchy today, aren't you? I didn't accuse you of interfering with my job, you know. In fact, I'm damned grateful you stepped in on a couple of those things."

Synnamon forced herself to relax. "You've been to the office already, then?"

"No, I called Carol from the airport." He rubbed the back of his neck and yawned.

"Then…" She knew she shouldn't say it, but the words slipped out before she could stop herself. "Then you haven't seen Nicole."

"No. Why?"

She hesitated, and then prevaricated. "Nothing I can put my finger on."

"But you obviously have a reason—and I'm interested in why you brought up Nick, because she left an odd message for me."

Synnamon's heart felt hollow.

"Something about a crisis at her other job keeping her away from Sherwood this week. I'm starting to wonder, myself, if she really wants to make the change."

"I couldn't possibly judge that." Synnamon toyed with the stack of tickets.

Conner didn't press the point. He reached for one of the bits of heavy bright red paper instead. "What's this?"

"Tickets to the Valentine's Have a Heart Ball."

"Do we really need a dozen of them?"

"Of course not," Synnamon said tartly. "In fact, I didn't plan on going at all, since we're hardly an advertisement for lovers. I'm selling them for Morea."

"Of course," he said. "I should have known."

She wished she could find even a hint of irony in his voice—a bit of sarcasm that she could twist into a belief that he cared—but he sounded perfectly straightforward.

The silence grew. She stacked the tickets neatly and didn't look at him. "How was your trip?"

"Just a business trip—pretty much like all of them. Got a few problems solved and discovered some new ones. Made one good deal, but a couple of others I'd hoped for didn't come through." His hand went to the back of his neck again.

Synnamon's hands ached to rub his muscles till the tension faded away and he was soothed into the rest he so obviously needed. But she no longer had the right to do that...

In fact, she told herself curtly, she'd never really had that right. Even in the early days, the best days, it had never been that sort of marriage, and it would be folly to forget it now. It would only cause more pain in the long run if she were to start editing her memories.

"You'd better get some sleep," she said. She knew her voice was curt, but she couldn't help it.

I'm glad he won't be here long, she told herself. *I hope Nicole doesn't waste any time.*

But that didn't ease the dull ache deep in her chest.

*   *   *

Conner looked better by the time Mrs. Ogden's turkey tetrazzini was ready to serve a couple of hours later. "Thanks for suggesting the nap," he said as he held Synnamon's chair. "I always did have trouble sleeping on airplanes. Even in first class there's really not enough room to get comfortable."

She served his portion and passed his plate across the table. "That's the bad side of being so tall, I suppose." Her voice was carefully casual. "You do look better."

You look wonderful, her heart said. Asleep or awake, rested or tired, sick or well—it wouldn't matter to her, now that she knew how she felt about him. He would always look wonderful.

"I expect it'll take me a couple of days to catch up at the office," Conner said. "But after that, perhaps we could declare an afternoon off and start to look for a house."

Synnamon's hand tightened on her fork. "I don't think that would be a good idea."

"Why not?"

She regretted letting her words outrun her brain. It had been the obvious answer, expecting as she did that by the end of the week he would have talked to Nicole and any house-hunting trip would be called off, anyway. But it might have been simpler and more sensible to agree instead of face the question. What reason could she give, really, for not wanting to go shopping?

She grasped at the first straw she thought of and said, "It's the slow season for real estate. It's hard to show houses in the winter, so—"

"Seems to me that makes it a buyer's market, if the whole world isn't looking along with us."

"But because of that, a lot of people wait till spring to put their homes up for sale."

Conner shrugged. "Well, if we don't find anything we like, we'll just keep looking. If the Hartfords are coming to Denver anytime soon, we'll need the space."

Synnamon couldn't stop herself. "I don't think that's such a good idea, either. Having them move up here, I mean."

Conner put down his fork. "What's gotten into you? They want to come, and we're going to need them."

She folded her hands in her lap, trying to stop her fingers from trembling.

"Are we back to this again?" He sounded more sad than annoyed. "If the next thing you're going to suggest is that I just get out of your life—"

She raised her chin a fraction. *Why not*? she asked herself. It would be far better to ask him to leave now than to wait around for him to end it. Her heart was dangling by a thread as it was—a thread that was more frayed by the moment. If she asked him to go, she could preserve a remnant of her dignity by making the split her choice, not his.

And even if he later found out that she'd known about Nicole and the baby... Well, at least Synnamon wouldn't have to be there. She wouldn't have to see him agonize, or hear him apologize. Or, worst of all, watch in frozen pain as he tried to hide his happiness.

She twisted her hands together till the ache in her fingers helped her deny the agony in her heart. "As a matter of fact, Conner," she said firmly, "why don't we just call it off right now?"

"I'd love to." His voice was cool. "I had a good chance to think this week, too. But that's hardly the question we're dealing with just now, is it? The fact is that as long as we share a child, I'm *in* your life, and there's no getting out. Believe me, if it wasn't for the baby—"

Synnamon's self-control snapped. It was bad enough to know that to him she was no more than an incubator, but for him to come straight out and say it hurt her beyond bearing. "Don't let that affect your choices," she snapped. "I only told you about the baby in the first place because it seemed the fair thing to do. If I'd had any idea what you'd expect me to put up with—"

"More than I should have expected, obviously, from a woman who's so cold that every time she exhales the furnace kicks on."

Synnamon was too furious to let herself admit the hurt that lay buried beneath her anger. "I might be cold around you, but that doesn't mean I *never* feel—"

"Synnamon, you don't know what warm is."

If there had been any pain in his voice—if it had been an accusation rather than a simple, flat statement—the charge might have hurt her less. But the fact that he not only found her unfeeling but so obviously didn't care wounded her like the thrust of a dull knife.

"Obviously I made the wrong choice," she said.

"About what? Telling me about the baby or not having an abortion? You aren't making things any easier for anyone by treating this baby like a life sentence, you know."

"Isn't that what you've made it? And there isn't even any chance of getting time off for good behavior!"

Conner pushed his chair from the table. "Oh, I wouldn't worry about that—since good behavior seems beyond us both these days."

Synnamon had no idea how long Mrs. Ogden had been standing in the doorway between foyer and living room, watching her. Finally the housekeeper cleared her throat, and Synnamon turned from her study of the hazy mountain range. "What is it, Mrs. Ogden?"

"I just wondered if you had any preference on the dinner menu for tonight."

"How about arsenic soup and foxglove salad?" She shook her head. "I'm sorry. I don't like being so sarcastic, but I can't seem to help it."

Mrs. Ogden made a comforting click with her tongue. "Now, now. You'll feel better once the morning sickness is all over. I remember with my first little one, I actually hated my husband for a while because it was his fault I felt so awful. But once the baby starts to move…"

Synnamon tuned her out. Somehow she doubted that the Ogdens, whatever their problems, had lived in the same sort of armed camp she and Conner had been occupying for the past few days. All her fingernails were gone, and if something didn't happen soon she'd probably start chewing her toes.

How long, she asked herself, was Nicole planning to keep the sword suspended above her head? And how long was Synnamon going to stand around and wait for it to drop?

"No longer," she said firmly.

"What?" Mrs. Ogden sounded a bit offended.

"Sorry. Excuse me, please—I just remembered something I have to do."

She called Annie at Sherwood, and said, "Do me a favor?"

"Anything, Mrs. Welles, you know that."

"Two favors, then," Synnamon said firmly. "I'm not your boss any more, so would you please use my first name? And second—I need to call Nicole Fox at her regular job, and I don't want to ask Carol for the number."

There was enough of the perfect secretary left in Annie that she didn't even ask why. "Let me put you on hold," she said, and a moment later Synnamon was reaching for a pen.

She stared at the number for several minutes before she picked up the phone again.

A bored-sounding secretary answered. ''Ms. Fox isn't in,'' she said. ''But she'll probably call later. Can I take a message?''

''No.'' Then Synnamon took a deep breath. ''Yes—and get this word for word, please. 'Synnamon Welles called to ask, Would you kindly do something about this situation you're in?' ''

The puzzled-sounding secretary repeated it, and Synnamon put the phone down. The tightness in her chest had eased, if only by a fraction. At least, now that she'd done the little she could, she didn't feel quite so helpless any more.

The dinner hour arrived, and Conner with it. He was almost painfully prompt these days, Synnamon had noted.

Mrs. Ogden had made pot roast. Obviously, Synnamon thought, she'd decided a little down-home atmosphere might help smooth things out. She was dishing their entrees up as they entered the dining room together, in silence.

''You don't need to stay to serve that,'' Synnamon said.

Mrs. Ogden didn't even glance up. ''It's quite all right. I just love seeing those sour looks you two give each other curdling my gravy.''

Synnamon bit her lip. Obviously her halfhearted excuse this afternoon hadn't sat well with Mrs. Ogden, and she'd have some fences to mend come tomorrow morning. Then there was the fact that Conner hadn't even seemed to notice the exchange. Mrs. Ogden's attitude didn't bode well, but Conner's was positively threatening.

If this keeps up, she thought, *we'll all be nuts.*

She had to force herself to pick at her dinner, and it wasn't until after she heard the back door close behind Mrs. Ogden that she made an effort to start a conversation. Then she pushed her untouched Bavarian cream aside and said, "Tough day?"

She thought for a moment that Conner wasn't going to answer.

"You might say so." He picked up his coffee. "Nick called this afternoon and dropped a bombshell on me."

A bombshell. So her message to Nicole had gotten through and jolted her—finally—into action.

Now that the moment she had been waiting for had arrived, all Synnamon wanted to do was run from it. Suddenly her throat was so tight the air felt too thick to breathe. The soft scent of half a dozen beeswax candles in the table centerpiece seemed as harsh and overpowering as a chemical fire.

"No wonder—" Her voice was little more than a breath. She cut the words off and picked up her water goblet.

"No wonder what?" Conner's gaze sharpened on her.

Synnamon shrugged. "I'd noticed that you were a bit moody when you came in." *And that*, she thought, *was an understatement that deserved a Pulitzer Prize!*

He sipped his coffee, watching her over the rim. "I thought perhaps you knew ahead of time."

She tried to sound interested but detached. "What was the bombshell?"

"She backed out of the job."

The words took an instant to register. Her muscles seemed to understand before her brain did, and with detached interest Synnamon watched her wrist turn and her fingers loosen, letting her goblet tumble to the table. She didn't even jump when the water surged over her, drenching the front of her dress.

She backed out of the job. But that made no sense at all.

Conner set his cup down. "You seemed shocked."

"So do you." She hardly heard what she said. It took the last air in her lungs to form the words. "But—you told me yourself you thought she was considering it."

"I may have said it, but I didn't really believe she'd do it. In fact, I can't believe it now." He was frowning.

It was not the reaction she had expected. It wasn't even close. She would not have been surprised at shock, pain, discomfort, confusion. But anger? Anger that obviously wasn't focused at her, but at Nicole—and not because of a baby, but because of a job.

She said, tentatively, "That's what you're angry about? The job?"

"Wouldn't you be? She hadn't actually signed an employment contract, but we'd agreed on the deal. I held the position to make it convenient for her past the time I wanted the job filled—and then she pulls this." He shook his head.

Synnamon was stunned. One thing was obvious. Nicole hadn't told him about the baby.

But why? What on earth could have made the woman decide to keep such a secret?

For Conner's sake, she thought. *To spare him pain.*

She could understand that. She'd considered doing the same thing herself, when she'd discovered her pregnancy. It wasn't Conner's fault or his responsibility, she'd told herself. Why tell him at all?

She'd ended up doing so, of course, for two reasons. One was her own moral code. She felt it was wrong not to tell the man he was to have a child. But equally important—even though she wouldn't have admitted it at the time—had been her selfish desire to win him back.

But what if her baby had been the second one? If the situation had been reversed, if he'd already known about Nicole's pregnancy before Synnamon had discovered hers, would she have told him?

No, she thought. *I wouldn't, because it would only cause him pain.*

Sadness swept over her. What a noble and generous decision Nicole had made. It was also dead wrong, of course, but noble nonetheless.

How odd it was, she thought, that in the midst of the whole mess she found herself thinking that the two of them—she and Nicole—could have been friends if things had only been different.

"Well?" Conner said.

Synnamon stood up and started to clear the table. "I'm sure she has her reasons," she said softly.

Conner watched her, his gaze brooding, and then abruptly pushed his chair back. In silence, he carried his dishes to the kitchen and then vanished down the hall toward the guest suite.

Synnamon slipped quietly past his door and closed herself into her own room.

No wonder Nicole had wanted time to think things through. But Synnamon, out of her own impatience, had left a curt message and perhaps pushed the woman into a decision she would later regret. Nicole had refused—for reasons that to her were obviously overwhelming—to interfere in an existing marriage.

But that's only going to make all three of us unhappy, Synnamon thought. The sheer weight of numbers dictated a different answer. If there could be two relatively happy people instead of three miserable ones...

She knew what she had to do.

She sat for a little while longer, trying to build up her willpower, and then she crossed the hall and knocked on the guest room door.

CHAPTER TEN

SYNNAMON knocked, but she didn't hear his step on the thick carpet. She raised her hand to knock again, and the door opened under her touch.

"Well." Conner folded his arms across his chest. "To what do I owe this honor?"

Tears prickled behind her eyes. She couldn't look at him. "I just wanted to say…" Her voice failed, and she had to clear her throat before she could start again. "I'm sorry for everything."

She didn't know how long the silence lasted. She only knew it seemed a hundred years—and even that wasn't long enough. Because the moment he answered, whether he accepted her apology or rejected it, she would have to go away from him, and that was the one thing she didn't want to do.

The tears began to overflow.

Conner didn't speak. He moved, instead, and held out his arms.

Synnamon tried to turn away, but her body wouldn't obey orders. She gave a little whimper and crept into his embrace. She knew it was foolish, stupid, *wrong*—but she could not deny herself a last bit of closeness.

"Oh, Synnamon," he said. He sounded as if he was in pain, too.

If she could have him just a little while longer, she told herself, just long enough to create one last cherished memory, then she would tell him that he could go, with her blessing, to Nicole.

Just a little while longer. Who would it hurt, after all?

She knew she was making excuses that might not stand up even to her own inspection in the light of day. But right now she didn't care. She would do what she had to do—and she had a sneaky suspicion that Nicole would understand.

Conner drew her ever so slightly closer, and Synnamon let herself relax until the softness of her body molded against the strength of his. Slowly, she raised her face to his and let her fingertips brush his cheek.

He had told her once to let him know when she changed her mind about wanting to make love with him. Now she told him, with every nonverbal means at her command. Simply being close to him brought pleasure. Touching him and being touched created glory.

When she gave herself to him, it was, for the first time ever, completely without hesitation, without reservation and with all the love she possessed.

One last loving, she told herself, *to hang onto for the rest of my life…*

And then there was no possibility of coherent thought—only sensation stronger than anything she had ever known. A beauty she had no more than glimpsed before unfolded for her in a panorama of surrealistic color and crashing sound and left her shaking and crying and clinging to him with all the frantic strength of her desire.

He held her afterward, and stroked her hair, and smoothed away her tears, and a long while later he said, "I think we have some things to talk about."

Synnamon tensed and shook her head. "Tomorrow," she whispered, and kissed him again. "Tomorrow."

He held her even after he went to sleep, and she lay in silence for a long while, pressed against his side, watching and listening. She memorized every angle of his face, the curve of each eyelash, the rhythm of his heartbeat.

She waited till the middle of the night to slip away from him. He murmured a little protest and then sank back into sleep, and she left him there and retreated to her bedroom to pack a few of her most precious belongings. She tried a dozen times to write a note, and ended up with three bare sentences.

It's better this way for all of us. Maybe you should talk to Nicole again. I'll be in touch when I can.

She didn't know how to sign it, so she didn't. She folded the page, wrote his name on the outside and left it propped against the coffeepot where he would see it first thing in the morning.

Then, very quietly, she closed the apartment door behind her. The doorman downstairs summoned a cab, but she waited till it was well away from the building before she told the cabby to take her to the airport.

She'd fit right in with all the early commuters, Synnamon thought, on the red-eye flight to Phoenix.

The Contessa had called it the city of new beginnings. Synnamon had hoped that would be true for her, as well, but as the days slid by she found herself doubting that her hopes could ever rise again from the ashes she had made of her life. Perhaps, she thought, once the baby became more real, she would find energy once more, and faith, and an optimistic eye for the future. But in the meantime, it took all the stamina she had just to call Morea and leave a message for her to refile the divorce papers.

The Hartfords were obviously worried about her. Mrs. Hartford cosseted her with every kind of food Synnamon had ever said she liked, and probably would have tucked her into bed each evening if Synnamon had allowed it.

After the first sleepless night, she moved to the Contessa's room. It might hold as many memories as the guest suite, but at least they were more manageable ones.

Still, she lay awake for hours each night while she sorted out the rubbish pile she'd made of her life. She understood now that it hadn't been reluctance to stay married that had prompted her to ask Conner for a divorce. It had been the fear of going on as she was, loving him but unloved in return. She had been afraid that someday he might leave her alone, as her father had, so she had prompted the split herself instead of waiting uncertainly for the day she was sure would come.

She understood, too, why she'd been so generous—despite Morea's strenuous and reasonable objections—in that first, abortive property settlement. By giving Conner full control of Sherwood, Synnamon had been setting him free. She'd separated herself from the company hoping, deep inside the hidden corners of her heart, that he would say the company didn't matter, that he wanted her as much as he wanted Sherwood. That he wanted her *more*...

But it hadn't happened that way, of course, and so she'd moved on. She'd resigned from her job and told herself and Conner and everyone who asked that she was escaping the stress of her father's legacy, the pressures of customer service.

She'd been trying to escape, all right. But it wasn't job stress she'd run from, it was Conner—and the knowledge, no less real even though she hadn't admitted it to herself at the time, that she could never be as important to him as he was to her.

How stupid, she thought. *I had almost everything I wanted, but I threw it away because I wanted more!* She'd had Conner, his name, his promise of fidelity, his honor.

But she'd wanted his love, so she'd tossed away the rest as if it had no value.

And now she had nothing at all.

There was no escaping Valentine's Day. It wasn't so much a day any more, Synnamon concluded in disgust, but an entire season. Long before February fourteenth, radio stations began blaring ads for flowers and candy. For a full week, the newspaper headlined the best places in Phoenix to buy exotic gifts, and one of the television talk shows featured daily interviews with the ten longest-married couples in the state. Red hearts and love songs were everywhere.

And it rained. Day after day it rained.

"Don't you dare complain about the rain," Morea said unsympathetically when she called on the twelfth, "because it's snowing like fury here in Denver. And as long as we've brought up fury, that's exactly how I feel about you. I'm speaking as your friend, of course, and not your attorney—but how dare you leave a message like that and then not even call back?"

"I'm sorry, Morea. I've been a little worn down."

"You could be more helpful, you know. You didn't tell my secretary where you are, you didn't even leave a number—"

"How did you find me, anyway? This phone is unlisted."

"It wasn't easy, let me tell you. I had to call Conner to get the number."

Synnamon's heart squeezed. "You didn't tell him I'm here?"

"How could I? I didn't know it myself. I just thought it was worth a try. In any case, if Phoenix was the first hideout I thought of, it's not likely to puzzle Conner for long.''

"Stupid question," Synnamon admitted.

Of course, Conner would have had no trouble figuring out where she'd gone. And the fact that he hadn't followed her, hadn't even called, only confirmed that it didn't matter to him what she did. By now he'd no doubt sorted everything out with Nicole.

"Now what's this about the divorce?" Morea asked. "Are we actually going through with it this time? Because if this is only another lovers' spat—''

"It's a far cry from that.''

"You know, I ought to refuse to take you back at all.''

"Please, Morea. I need a friend.''

"You know all my weaknesses, don't you?" Morea sighed. "I suppose we have to start from scratch with the property settlement. And now there'll be child support to negotiate, too.''

"No. I don't want any of that. Offer Conner the same deal we agreed to before on the property, and tell him I don't expect anything from him.''

"Are you out of your ever-loving *mind*?''

"No," Synnamon said calmly. "I think I've just started to get it back.''

Morea groaned. "You're already assured of a place in the hall of fame for difficult clients, Synnamon, you don't have to go for a world's record. All right, I'll get everything organized, and you can sign the papers Friday night at the Valentine's ball. Then if Conner agrees—''

"Now who's lost her marbles? If you think I'm coming back to Denver for a *dance*—''

"Of course you are," Morea interrupted. "The Have a Heart committee is giving you an award for selling the most tickets any one person's ever managed to peddle. How will it look if you don't show up to accept it?''

Synnamon managed a groan—which Morea seemed to interpret as agreement—put the telephone down and went out on the terrace. The rain was only a light mist now, and under the shelter of the terrace roof the air was clean and fresh and almost warm, compared to what she'd left behind in Colorado. She stretched out on a chaise longue and watched scattered raindrops splashing into the pool just off the terrace.

All right, she decided. She'd go to the ball, since Morea apparently was going to insist. She'd make just enough of an appearance to keep the committee happy, she'd sign the papers, and then she'd come back to Phoenix and get on with life. It was time to stop feeling sorry for herself, for her sake and that of her child.

She didn't quite know how she'd start. With simple things, she supposed—a swim, a walk, a little shopping, a call to a friend. The important thing was to begin. If she went through the motions long enough, surely some-day she'd feel like living again.

The grand ballroom of the Denver Kendrick Hotel was agleam when Synnamon slipped through the main doors and edged off to a shadowed corner. From this isolated spot, nearly concealed behind a trellis draped with roses and ivy, she could see most of the enormous room. Three huge crystal chandeliers, their multitude of tiny bulbs dimmed, cast a romantic glow over the crowd of dancers. Around the edges of the polished dance floor were rows of tiny tables draped in pink linen, each topped with a single long-stemmed red rose in a glass vase. Red and pink balloons drifted in the shifting air currents. From a stage at one end of the ballroom came the soft strains of a love ballad.

Perfect, Synnamon thought. The ball was well under-way, just as she'd planned. The ballroom was a sea of red and pink and white dresses. Her soft pink gown, flattering as it was, wouldn't be noticed from a distance. She could lose herself in the crowd, and no one would know how long she'd been there.

The moment her part was played, she could vanish just as easily. Since she was staying in the hotel, she didn't have to retrieve a wrap. All she had to do was slip up the stairs from the mezzanine to the next floor as if she was seeking out a ladies' room, then vanish into the closest elevator and to her room. No one would miss her, and she could be on a plane to Phoenix first thing tomorrow morning.

It was ironic, though, she thought, to find herself staying even for a single night in the hotel that had been Conner's headquarters during their separation. She wondered which room had been his in those long weeks. Had he been comfortable here?

And was he comfortable now? She wondered if he was with Nicole tonight, celebrating this day for lovers. Perhaps he was remembering, as Synnamon was, that if everything had gone according to plan, their divorce would have been final today. They'd be finished with it now, instead of having to start all over.

Stop thinking about that, she told herself, *and start looking for Morea*.

A voice came from behind her. "Happy anniversary."

She turned too fast, and the slender heel of her shoe skidded on the hardwood floor. Conner's hand closed on her elbow, steadying her till she could regain her balance. Then he took half a step back, as if to better inspect her.

What was she supposed to say? Thanks for the good wishes? It would be an idiotic response, but then his greeting had been, too. He didn't sound happy, and he certainly didn't look happy. His jaw was tight, and his eyes were turbulent.

But he still looked marvelous, she thought. His tuxedo fitted like a dream, and the snowy white of his pleated shirt made him look as if he'd just returned from a few days in the sun. For all she knew, of course, he might have. The thought of him lounging on a beach somewhere with Nicole sent a stab of envy through her heart.

Conner's voice was crisp. ''I thought you said you didn't intend to come to this affair.''

Synnamon shrugged. ''Morea put the pressure on. You know how she can be. I didn't realize you were coming, either.''

''Or you'd have warned me to stay away? It's just as well, anyway. You've saved me a trip to Phoenix.''

She blinked in surprise.

''You look puzzled. Have you forgotten about that talk we didn't finish?''

Synnamon let her gaze drift across the crowded ballroom. ''Well, we can hardly do it here and now, can we?''

''Why not?''

''Oh, come on, Conner. You've known all this time where I was, so why didn't you just pick up the phone if you had something to say?''

''Because by the time Morea told me you'd moved to start the divorce all over again, you were already on your way here.''

She sighed. ''I'm not going to talk about it right now, Conner.''

''Nobody's paying any attention.''

That was true enough, she reflected. They were probably as alone in this corner of the ballroom, even though they were surrounded by five hundred people, as it was possible to be. The dancers' attention was focused on the music. The spectators were watching the dancers. No one was paying attention to the isolated corners.

"All right," she said. "Let's get it over with. Surely you can't mean you're surprised that I've filed for divorce again. Why did you think I left, anyway?"

"Because you needed some time to think—even though you did tell me that we'd talk the next day. Or was that just an out-and-out lie? An excuse so you could get away?"

The accusation was close enough to the truth that she couldn't stop the embarrassed flush that rose in her cheeks.

"At any rate," Conner went on, "that's why I didn't hop on the next plane after you. I thought, once you'd had some distance, a chance to consider... And as long as we're asking why, I've got one, too. If you were planning to leave, why did you practically beg to go to bed with me that night? Was it just a nice little farewell gesture? A goodbye gift?"

The accusing note in his voice made Synnamon's heart twist.

"Were you trying to soothe your conscience by giving me something to remember?"

"No!" she snapped.

"Well, that's some comfort, at least. Unless you mean you did it because you finally decided I wasn't so bad in bed after all, and you wanted one last thrill to remember."

Tears of pain came to her eyes. He was making her precious memory sound unbearably stupid and cheap.

"Please, Conner. Going over it all won't do any good." She braced herself. "Did you take my advice?"

"Which bit of it?"

"About talking to Nicole."

"Otherwise known as the spanner in the works? What about her?"

His tone was curt. It was unlike him, Synnamon thought, to be so callous. Upset, certainly. Angry, perhaps. But not uncaring. Not Conner...

"You don't need to be cruel," she said. "What are you going to do about her?"

"I don't have much choice, do I? I'll look for someone else to handle the research and development job."

Synnamon was stunned, and the question was out before she could stop herself. "Then she still hasn't told you about the baby?" She caught her breath, but it was too late.

"Of course she did." He sounded impatient. "That's why she's going back to her other job, because it's less complex. It's also less money, which is why she dithered around so long before making up her mind. But she'll have more freedom for the baby."

The music shifted to a soft and sensual love song, and the ballroom seemed to hush as the dancers slowed to the new rhythm. Synnamon could hear the rustle of air in the balloons above her head. But where Conner's voice was concerned, her hearing seemed abruptly scrambled. He couldn't possibly be saying what she thought she had heard.

"That's all it means to you?" she whispered.

"Why should it..." His gaze sharpened on her face. "Oh, no. You don't think—you can't think Nick's baby has anything to do with me."

"Doesn't it?" she asked crisply.

"No, it doesn't. Nick has a perfectly inadequate jerk of a lover who isn't worth the dust on her shoes. He can't even hold a job, which is why she was so torn between coming to Sherwood and staying where she was.''

''And Fargo? You were there together.''

''What about it? I needed help. She came up and gave it. She also cried on my shoulder a lot about how sick she was of the boyfriend's behavior. And I—'' He stopped.

Synnamon said softly, ''You told her how sick you were of me, I suppose?''

''I did my share of crying on shoulders—in a manner of speaking. But that's as far as it went, I swear. My God, Synnamon, what kind of Lothario do you think I am?''

She shook her head. ''It's all right, Conner. Don't think I don't understand, because I do. Our marriage was over, all but the paperwork. Why shouldn't you be seeing someone else? And Nicole told me herself...''

But Nicole hadn't actually said that Conner was the father of her baby, Synnamon realized.

I assumed that because I loved him so much, she must too. I assumed that no woman could overlook him, that no woman could prefer another man if Conner was around. And if she loved him, then of course her baby would be his, as well.

Her stomach was churning. She'd had evidence of Nicole's love, she told herself frantically. She'd never forget the look in Nicole's face that day she'd stopped by the apartment with flowers and told Synnamon what a lucky woman she was. Nicole had meant every word of it. There had been no mistaking the love in her eyes.

And maybe she did love Conner, Synnamon thought. The boyfriend might be no more than a poor substitute for the man she couldn't have. Or maybe the love Nicole felt was a different kind than Synnamon knew but, blinded by her own experiences and prejudices, Synnamon had been unable to distinguish the difference.

"I assumed she *must* love you," she said, almost to herself, "because I did."

Conner might as well have turned to bronze. Not an eyelash twitched.

The music shifted once again, but Synnamon didn't hear it. The realization of what she had said and the implications of that admission crept over her like a cold mist, soaking slowly into her bones. "Not that it changes anything, of course."

Conner moved then, shifting his feet like a boxer about to leave his corner. He put his hands on his hips. *"Did?"* he asked quietly.

She had to go back over what she'd said before she quite understood the question, and then she was forced to admit a grudging respect for the way he'd gone, with a single word, straight to the heart of the matter.

She was already aching from the strain. Surely it couldn't get any worse—unless he were to pry. So why not admit the truth, and at least not add the pain of cross-examination? "No," she said quietly. "I didn't mean past tense. I meant present."

She listened to his long, slow intake of breath and the even longer release. Was he counting to ten, she wondered, or did he have to go even higher? "Is that why you ran away? Because you—" the calmness in his voice gave way for an instant "—love me?"

Synnamon didn't look at him. "Too much to keep you miserable. If Nicole was your happiness…" She stopped, then said, very softly, "Then I wanted you to be happy."

"She's not. We've been friends—no more."

"At any rate, that's sort of beside the point now, isn't

it?'' Synnamon turned restlessly from him, staring unsee-ing through the trellis to the ballroom floor.

She couldn't face him. The mere act of looking at him would make it far more difficult to say what she needed to—and it was desperately important that he understand.

''Beside the point,'' she said huskily, ''because I don't think I can do what you want, Conner. I can't live with you, and love you, and know the only value I have for you is the baby. What if it's not the son you want? I couldn't stand to see my little girl rejected as I was—''

He hadn't moved, but she could feel his anger pounding over her as strongly as the sudden hard-rock beat of the band.

His voice was low and rough. ''Dammit, Synnamon, I am not your father—and if Silas was still alive, I could cheerfully kill him for what he's done to you.''

The cold fury in his voice sent ice chips up her spine.

''I'm sorry,'' she managed. ''But it's always been so clear that you were only interested in Sherwood....'' Her voice trailed off.

''Sherwood,'' he said finally, ''was an attraction.''

''Tell me something I didn't know.'' Her tone was bit-ter.

''So were you, in a very distant kind of way. You're eye-catching, Synnamon. Beautiful, yes—but it's more than that. The way you carry yourself and the air of mys-tery that hangs around you...'' He sighed. ''But you were so chilly I didn't seriously consider even trying to get to know you until your father suggested I take you to that party.''

''Please, Conner,'' she begged. ''Don't give me the de-tails. I really don't want to know how you fixed it up between you.''

He didn't seem to hear. ''But there was something different about you that night, when I watched you with the employees—not the management team you worked with all the time, but the line workers, the packers, the kids in the shipping department. And I wanted to find out if there was a real woman under that frosty shell.''

She turned slowly to face him, eyes wide.

''That was when I really started watching you and falling for you—but I didn't want to face up to that. It was too painful to admit that I'd tumbled headlong into love with a woman who didn't care if I existed.''

Tumbled into love? She couldn't breathe.

''Who only married me to get away from her father—''

''I didn't, really.'' She could barely whisper.

''You did a good job of faking it, then. You didn't care if it was me in your bed or a stuffed teddy bear—except that the teddy bear would be less demanding and a whole lot more fun to sleep with.''

She felt embarrassed color rise in her cheeks. ''That's not true. I never rejected you—''

''No, you didn't,'' he said dryly. ''You acted as though you had no say in the matter. You were such a lady in bed that I felt like a criminal every time I thought of making love to you.'' Conner cleared his throat. ''The first time I ever felt you wanted me—really wanted *me*—was the night the Contessa died.''

''I was so lonely that night,'' she admitted.

''But the next morning, you were right back to being the perfect lady. *Thanking* me—my God, Synnamon, you don't know how that hurt. And giving my rings back—''

''I hated the idea that you might be sorry for me. Maybe even feel bound to me because we'd made love.'' She put one hand to her temple. Her head was spinning. ''Is that why you moved to the guest suite? When we were still together, I mean.''

"You call that being together?" he asked dryly. "Of course that's why. I wanted you so much, and it was a little easier that way."

"I thought you'd gotten tired of me." Her body was trembling. "That I hadn't pleased you."

With two steps, Conner was beside her, taking her weight against him. "And I thought you were relieved when I didn't bother you any more."

She shook her head violently and clung to him. "My father taught one lesson well," she said bitterly. "You're only loved for what you can give."

"And since you couldn't be the son he wanted, he found you worthless." He held her a few inches from him and looked intently at her. "What is it going to take to convince you that *I am not Silas*? I don't care if this baby is a boy or a girl. I don't care if there's a baby at all." He paused. "Yes, I do care. If you'd aborted our child—".

"I could never do that."

"I know that now. Anyway, it isn't the baby that matters most. It's you I love, Synnamon. So much that having to face the fact that I couldn't reach you, that my love wasn't enough to break through that wall around you, almost drove me crazy."

She put her head on his shoulder. "Don't, Conner."

"Maybe it's better if I tell you all of it, sweetheart."

She considered, and nodded. He pulled her closer and laid his cheek against the top of her head. His voice, soft and level, stirred her hair.

"To protect myself, I became distant and cold and uncaring. The day you asked for the divorce, it was almost a relief. At least it was over, and I could finally admit that I was a failure at the most important thing I'd ever tried to do."

She held him tight, wanting to tell him that he wasn't

the one who had failed. But her voice was incoherent. It was the closeness of their bodies, the warmth of their embrace that eventually soothed them both. She sensed his muscles relaxing and felt her tension easing away.

A long while later, he raised his cheek from her hair and said, "Will you wear my rings again, Synnamon?"

She nodded, and was startled when he shifted slightly and reached into the breast pocket of his tux to pull them out.

"I never bothered to put them back in the safe," he admitted. "Sometimes they've been a reminder of unbearable pain, sometimes of a moment when I really believed we had a chance. But always a reminder of you."

"I know," she said. "You said the diamond was perfect—hard and cold, and just like me."

"But always with the flash of fire," he said softly, "and the promise of warmth that could keep a man content forever—if I could only reach you and free it."

"I wouldn't have blamed you for writing me off altogether." The knowledge of how close she had come to disaster, through her misguided efforts at self-protection, made her feel sick. "If it hadn't been for the baby…"

"I don't know what I'd have done," he admitted. "I expect I'd have tried again anyway—because even with my pride in shreds, I couldn't put you out of my mind. And what did I have left to lose?"

He cuddled her closer, and Synnamon let her body melt into his. She'd never known what a comfort it was simply to be held. There was one nice thing about the shadowed corners of a formal ballroom, she thought hazily. The casual observer wouldn't even notice whether a couple was dancing or just embracing.

It was a long while before she remembered that while they'd solved the most important problem, others still awaited attention. "What *are* you going to do about research and development?" she asked. "Look for someone else?"

"I don't want to," he said slowly. "The department has already been without a head for too long. If Nick had procrastinated any longer there wouldn't be anything left."

"No wonder you were grouchy all the time."

"That, along with not knowing where I stood with you from minute to minute." He smiled at her. "I suppose I might have been a little testy."

"A little?" She leaned more comfortably against him.

"Actually," Conner said, "I was thinking I might hire myself. I like research and development, and I miss my lab."

Synnamon frowned. "But can you do it all? Now that I have you back, I'd sort of like to see you once in a while. It's not my decision, of course, but—"

"But you're always sensitive to what's best for Sherwood."

"Well, of course I'm interested."

He smiled. "Don't be touchy, darling—that was a compliment. I was wondering if you might consider a change, too. If you were to come back to work as the head of the whole place…"

"Me?" Her voice was little more than a squeak.

"Of course. You're meant for it, Synnamon. Silas couldn't see it, but he trained you for the job despite himself. You've shown it in a dozen ways. You saw immediately that Nick wasn't right for the job—"

"That," she said wryly, "was mostly because I was jealous."

"Still, you recognized the fact long before I did. And you told me exactly how to handle Luigi."

"True. I'm apparently only blind where you're concerned."

Conner grinned. "And you took care of things while I was in Asia. Carol kept me posted."

"You were thinking of this then?"

"Oh, yes—until I came home to the coldest hello a man ever got."

Synnamon bit her lip.

"Followed by the warmest night of our marriage. That's the thing that hurt worst, actually—to think that you could hold me like that, make love with me, then leave that icy little note and walk away."

Tears were stinging her eyes. "I thought it would kill me to give you up."

"Good." He kissed her softly. "Remember that—so you're never tempted to try it again."

Her tears overflowed, and gently he kissed each one away. After a couple of minutes, however, Synnamon started laughing and tried to push him away.

His arms tightened around her. "What's the matter? Am I tickling you?"

"No—but you have mascara all over you." She traced the line of his lips with her fingertip.

Conner frowned. "I thought you wore the kind that won't come off."

"Well, you guaranteed it against water aerobics, rainstorms and lifeboat rescues—not tears of joy. Obviously, we'll need more tests. Since I'm the boss now—"

He didn't wait for her to finish. "And just as obviously, we can't make an official appearance at the ball with mascara all over us."

"Oh. That *is* a problem, isn't it? I have a room upstairs."

"An inspired idea if I ever heard one." Conner's lips

were against her throat, and his breath teased the pulse point under her ear. "You know, I like your suggestion of putting a bed in the president's office, too."

"Even if it's a baby crib?"

"Well, I suppose it'll do for now." He drew her closer yet.

A couple of minutes later, Synnamon emerged from the most thorough kiss she'd ever dreamed of and murmured, "Morea will never forgive me when I tell her this."

"Of course she will. Who'll sell all the tickets for the Valentine's Ball next year if she holds a grudge?"

Synnamon laughed. "But we were going to have the perfect divorce. What a pity we had to go and mess it up!"

"But you're wrong, my love," Conner said firmly. "We're still going to have the perfect divorce."

She pulled away from him, eyes wide with shock.

He tugged a long-stemmed red rose out of the vine-draped trellis, folded her fingers around the stem and raised her hand to his lips. "Because," he said, "the perfect divorce for us is…no divorce at all."

And as he drew her gently into his arms, Synnamon smiled and agreed.

*   *   *   *   *

MILLS & BOON®

Makes
any time special

Enjoy a romantic novel from
Mills & Boon®

Presents™ *Enchanted*™ *Temptation*®

Historical Romance™ *Medical Romance*™

MILLS & BOON®

Next Month's Romance Titles

♡

Each month you can choose from a wide variety of romance novels from Mills & Boon®. Below are the new titles to look out for next month from the Presents™ and Enchanted™ series.

Presents™

THE MARRIAGE DECIDER — Emma Darcy
TO BE A BRIDEGROOM — Carole Mortimer
HOT SURRENDER — Charlotte Lamb
THE BABY SECRET — Helen Brooks
A HUSBAND'S VENDETTA — Sara Wood
BABY DOWN UNDER — Ann Charlton
A RECKLESS SEDUCTION — Jayne Bauling
OCCUPATION: MILLIONAIRE — Alexandra Sellers

Enchanted™

A WEDDING WORTH WAITING FOR — Jessica Steele
CAROLINE'S CHILD — Debbie Macomber
SLEEPLESS NIGHTS — Anne Weale
ONE BRIDE DELIVERED — Jeanne Allan
A FUNNY THING HAPPENED… — Caroline Anderson
HAND-PICKED HUSBAND — Heather MacAllister
A MOST DETERMINED BACHELOR — Miriam Macgregor
INTRODUCING DADDY — Alaina Hawthorne

On sale from 5th March 1999

H1 9902

Available at most branches of WH Smith, Tesco, Asda, Martins, Borders, Easons, Volume One/James Thin and most good paperback bookshops

FREE!

4 Books
and a surprise gift!

We would like to take this opportunity to thank you for reading this Mills & Boon® book by offering you the chance to take FOUR more specially selected titles from the Enchanted™ series absolutely FREE! We're also making this offer to introduce you to the benefits of the Reader Service™ —

- ★ FREE home delivery
- ★ FREE gifts and competitions
- ★ FREE monthly Newsletter
- ★ Books available before they're in the shops
- ★ Exclusive Reader Service discounts

Accepting these FREE books and gift places you under no obligation to buy; you may cancel at any time, even after receiving your free shipment. Simply complete your details below and return the entire page to the address below. *You don't even need a stamp!*

YES! Please send me 4 free Enchanted books and a surprise gift. I understand that unless you hear from me, I will receive 6 superb new titles every month for just £2.40 each, postage and packing free. I am under no obligation to purchase any books and may cancel my subscription at any time. The free books and gift will be mine to keep in any case.

N9EB

Ms/Mrs/Miss/Mr ....Initials ....

BLOCK CAPITALS PLEASE

Surname ....

Address ....

....Postcode ....

Send this whole page to:
THE READER SERVICE, FREEPOST CN81, CROYDON, CR9 3WZ
(Eire readers please send coupon to: P.O. BOX 4546, DUBLIN 24.)